NOTHING BUT A DRIFTER

NOTHING BUT A DRIFTER

Lee Hoffman

SAGEBRUSH
Large Print Westerns

First published in Great Britain by Hale
First published in the United States by Doubleday

Published in Large Print 2008 by ISIS Publishing Ltd.,
7 Centremead, Osney Mead, Oxford OX2 0ES
United Kingdom
by arrangement with
Golden West Literary Agency

The moral right of the author has been asserted

British Library Cataloguing in Publication Data
Hoffman, Lee, 1932–
    Nothing but a drifter. – Large print ed. –
    (Sagebrush western series)
    1. Western stories
    2. Large type books
    I. Title
    813.5'4 [F]

ISBN 978–0–7531–8012–9 (hb)

Printed and bound in Great Britain by
T. J. International Ltd., Padstow, Cornwall

CHAPTER
ONE

At last, Brian had come out of the snow-crusted high peaks of Ade's Ridge. The shaggy Texas mustang that had brought him through was gaunted now, and so was he. The tattered bedroll and warbag lashed behind his cantle held little grain, and even less grub for a man. It had been a hard ride. But now the worst of it was behind him.

Now he rode gentle slopes. Slopes flecked with forests of quaking aspen. Slopes sprouting new grass. Spring had reached into the valleys. It was turning the land green. The streams that meandered through the gullies had become gouts of thrashing thaw waters. The low ground was soggy. In some places it was fetlock-deep with runoff. The hollows were becoming bogs. It made for slow going in places, but it was a damn sight better than the sheer rock and thick snows on Ade's Ridge.

He rode easy, letting his mount pick its own way. The horse was a red roan gelding, a small wiry rawhide-bottomed mustang that could thrive on bark and thorns. But there had been no bark and thorns on Ade's Ridge. The horse was as worn now as Brian himself, aching for a good rest and a decent feed. For better than two weeks Brian had struggled the roan through the high peaks, through the rocks and snow, hunting a way past the avalanche that had buried the trail, and his pack horse with it.

The roan's ears flopped as it plodded along across a shallow gully that still held snow cupped in it, then up a slope slick with wet new grass. Atop the slope, Brian drew rein. He saw people ahead.

The ridge sloped into a broad basin. There were two riders well over to the far side. One was just dropping a loop on a crook-horned brindle steer. The steer was mired belly-deep in a boghole. It didn't appreciate the help at hand. It tossed its head, trying to duck the rope that spun toward it.

The loop closed on the steer's horns. The roper had the bitter end tied hard. The rope horse was a zebra dun under a Texas-style double-barrel saddle. Hoofs planted, the dun leaned on the rope. Its head was down and its ears flattened with determination.

The rider on the dun's back was bundled in a plaid blanket coat and batwing chaps, topped off with a flat black Stetson. At first glance, Brian thought it was a boy not yet filled out to man-size. At second look, he was certain it was a woman. Shifting in the saddle to rest his legs, he watched curiously. She had set a neat loop.

The second rider, on a round-rumped bay, dropped from his saddle. He looked middle-aged, built broad and solid. He was wearing a short-tailed hide jumper like a brush-popper, but wide batwings and a Stetson creased highcountry style, like the girl's. He stripped out of the chaps and threw them over his saddle. The bay shied as he did it. Holding the reins up at the bit with one hand, he used the other to pull off his spurs. He hung them on the saddle horn. Leaving the bay tied to a low bush, he waded into the bog.

The steer tried to hook him. But the girl's lass rope held the big crook-horned head firm. Knee-deep in the bog, the man began to paw at the mud trapping the steer.

Brian had fought bogged cattle often enough himself. He knew it was a hard, messy job. The mud could suck a struggling animal down like quicksand and hold it tight as a bear trap. If a cow was bogged for long, it grew weak from fighting the mud. If it weren't freed in time, it would die from exhaustion.

This steer hadn't been bogged long. It still had strength and courage. Wanting to fight the man digging it out, it pulled hard against the rope holding its head. At the jerk, the roping horse slipped on the hoof-churned mud. For an instant the steer had slack. It swung its horns at the man. But the horse caught footing again quickly. Hoofs set, it tightened the rope. Not too hard or it could pull the horns right off the steer's head, maybe break its neck. Not too easy, or the steer might get slack again.

The horse seemed to know its business. So did the girl with the lass rope. Brian shoved aside a passing thought about offering help. He was weary as hell, and they seemed able to manage without him.

The man dug the steer's front legs out first. Then he moved back to scoop mud away from a hind leg. When the steer felt the mud around that leg loosen, it tried to kick the man. The leg came free.

The dun leaned on the rope. The man pawed mud away from the other hind leg. The steer began to move. Floundering in the mud, it inched forward at the pull of the rope. As its hocks came clear, it tried to kick. It slipped in the slick goo and suddenly slammed down on its side. The rope horse halted, holding the line taut.

The man in the bog was half mired now himself. He struggled a boot out, took a step, and shoved at the steer's rump. The girl eased back the dun. The steer was free enough to slide. Dragged on the rope, pushed from behind, it moved slowly from the bog onto the new grass. Clear of the mud at last, it stopped fighting. It lay still on the ground, sides heaving as it gasped breath.

The man gestured and spoke. Brian couldn't hear his words at the distance, but the gestures were clear. He wanted the rope. The girl slacked it and recovered her loop. She backed her mount well away from the downed steer, built a new loop, and rolled it down the rope toward the man. He caught it and braced against it to drag himself out of the bog.

Half stumbling, he got himself onto solid ground. His legs were thick with mud to the thighs. His shoulders slumped wearily as he stood looking at the steer. It was just lying there, making no effort to rise. Free of the mud and able to survive, it seemed to have given up.

The girl collected her rope and held it ready as the man stiff-legged over to the steer's rump. He grabbed

4

the tail and gave a twist. The steer snorted. The man twisted. Thrashing, the steer got itself onto its belly. Its rump rose. It knelt a moment, its head hanging heavily. Then the front end began to come up. As it did, the man let go the tail and backed off.

Suddenly the steer was on its feet. And hooking. It lunged like a strike of lightning, swinging that big-horned head at the man.

The man jumped.

The girl loosed her loop at the steer's head.

They were quick. But not quick enough. The crooked horn swept across the man's gut. He staggered back. His hands clutched his belly as he fell.

As the girl's loop jerked tight on the steer's neck, the girl was wheeling her mount. It jumped jackrabbit, snapping the rope taut. The steer slammed to the ground.

She swung off the horse and raced to the fallen man.

Brian had thrown his horse into a gallop as he saw the steer hook. With the dark feeling that maybe his help would have prevented this, he plunged across the basin.

The girl was kneeling at the man's side. She looked up as she heard Brian's horse approaching. Her eyes were wide, blazing as if with fever.

"He's been gored!" she shouted.

"I saw," Brian called back. As he reached her, he jerked rein and dropped from the saddle. Even as his thoughts centered on the injured man, a part of his mind was on the girl, curious and appraising.

Her face was oval, fine-boned and delicate and young. Very young. She had none of the pale, painted prettiness of a saloon girl. The sun had tanned her skin and was putting fine squint lines around her eyes, giving her face a kind of boyishness.

Something about that face caught him. He wanted to stare at it. He wanted to probe behind it, to know who she was, this cowboy-woman.

Hunkering at her side, he concentrated on the injured man. "How bad is it?"

She shook her head, not knowing.

The man lay on his back. His eyes were open. They aimed at Brian. His body trembled and his voice came as a groan. "It ain't bad. Just help me up onto my horse."

"The hell." Brian touched a hand to the man's shoulder, saying with it for him to lie still. "You take it easy, mister."

"It ain't bad," the man repeated. But his look and voice denied his words. His face was clenched with pain, ashy white and slick with the sudden sweat of shock. There was blood seeping around the muddy hands he held jammed over the wound.

"Let me see," Brian said.

The hands slipped away. Brian bent to examine the wound. Faintly, the man said, "Texican?"

Brian wondered if it had been his way of speaking or his rig that told his origin. Likely both. Nodding, he said, "Pecos country. Name's Brian."

Taut-jawed, working to put sound into the words, the injured man told him, "I'm Sam Pearson. From down near the Nueces."

"We're both a long ways from home." Brian jerked off his gloves. Pearson's horsehide jumper was ripped at the waist. He opened it, then the vest under it. Pearson wore a faded blue shirt. It was smeared with a heavy stain of red. The stain spread down to his blue canvas pants. The pants were ripped through the waistband. As Brian began to unbutton Pearson's fly, he glanced at the girl. If she was shy about such things, she was too concerned to give it mind. Likely she was Pearson's wife, Brian thought, and the thought sent a surge of sadness through him.

He turned down the waist of the pants and shoved aside the shirttails. Under them, Pearson was wearing one-piece longhandles. The blood on them was bad, red and wet and spreading. Brian slipped the buttons and turned back the edges of ripped flannel from the torn flesh.

The steer's horn had hooked in just above Pearson's left hip, just clear of the bone at the socket. Angling upward, it had plowed flesh and pulled out again just a hair short of the point of the breast bone. The hole was welling blood.

At the sight of it, the girl flinched and gasped. Her face went so pale under its tan that Brian thought she was going to faint. He started to grab her. But she sucked a deep steadying breath and held on. Thinly, she said, "It's bad . . ."

"Maybe not so bad as it looks," Brian told her. He felt almost disappointed that she hadn't fainted. His arms felt empty for the lack of catching her in them, and holding her. Keeping his eyes on Pearson, he said, "It ain't too deep. I don't think his lights got damaged."

"But the blood? So much blood!"

"I got plenty to spare," Pearson mumbled. He sounded weak as hell. Brian thought he really couldn't spare a lot more.

"Can't we stop the bleeding?" the girl was asking.

"I reckon we'd better." Brian glanced around. "Snow. You got a wipe?"

She nodded. The bandana was under her collar, protecting her neck. She fingered it out.

"Go find some clean snow. There's plenty of it back the way I came," he said. "Pack your wipe full and fetch it here quick."

Nodding, she started for her horse. The lass rope tied hard to the dun's saddle was still holding the steer stretched on the ground. Rather than free the steer, she veered toward the bay. It tossed its head, showing white around the eyes, as she untied the reins. Its flattened ears told her it meant to get its head down and show her a few kinks. She was in too much of a hurry to play games. Instead of working it out easy, she got a tight cheek on the bridle, gave the horse a kick in the gut, and swung aboard.

The bay tried to pump under her. She had its head pulled around far enough to ruin its balance. Her concern for the injured man gave her the strength to hold it there. She had her seat in the saddle before the horse managed to straighten out. Setting her belly hooks firm in the cinch, she slapped the bay's flanks with the rein ends.

8

This was rougher handling than the horse was used to. Startled, it took off at a gallop, humping with each stride. The girl stayed close to the saddle. After a few futile tries at unseating her, the bay settled. She whipped the gallop into a run and headed back along Brian's trail.

Brian watched, impressed.

She was well out of earshot when Pearson worked up voice and asked Brian, "How bad is it really?"

"I've seen men hurt worse."

"I've seen them spill their guts out on the ground. Generally they died of it."

"You ain't dead yet. You got a doctor in these parts?"

"Sort of. Good horse doctor, does people too if need be. Two days' riding."

"Going and coming?"

"Each way."

That was bad, Brian thought. Too damned long. But he said, "Wouldn't hurt none to fetch him out for a look."

"I ain't sure I can wait," Pearson groaned.

"Not here. We'll have to fetch you home. Keep that hole clean and keep the rest of the blood inside you until the doc can take over," Brian said. "Your place far from here?"

"Yonder a ways. About three miles." Pearson indicated direction with a dart of his eyes.

Brian scanned the stands of quaking aspens on the slopes. "We can rig a travvy for you."

"I'm obliged. I'm lucky you come along when you did."

"I'm sorry I didn't come sooner and lend you a hand with that steer."

"That damned ornery son-of-a-bitch! I should have pulled his damned horns off for a hatrack instead of booting him out that bog!" Anger gave a brief strength to Pearson's voice.

Brian nodded toward the steer. "You want it beefed?"

"Hell no! I got venison hanging at home. I mean to market that bastard. Let him take a long walk and put some coin in my poke before he gets his throat cut, damn him!"

Brian grinned. This man was all cowman, pure Texican, rawhide enough to hold a man's respect. Evidently he wasn't just a hired hand but owner of the brand the steer wore. A forked P, with swallowtails right and left for earmarks. P for Pearson.

Brian told him, "Day before yesterday I killed a calf I reckon was yours. Blue meat. Sucking a Forked P cow."

"For the meat?" Pearson asked.

"Uh-huh. I've been riding hungry. It was the first meat I could set my sights on in nigh a week."

"You're welcome to it. All you want. I got better at home though. My Hildy spreads a stout table. Glad to have you stay a piece." The anger faded from Pearson's voice, leaving it little more than painful breath. He sounded as if he were sinking into exhaustion.

It might be better to keep him talking than let him fall into silent brooding, Brian thought. He asked, "Hildy your missus?"

"Uh-huh. She's a good woman. Hell of a good woman. Deserves better than me."

The girl had topped the ridge and was coming on fast, holding out a stuffed bandana in one hand. She had the feisty bay completely under control. With a nod toward her, Brian said, "Here she comes now."

For a moment, puzzlement mingled with the pain on Pearson's face. Then he cracked his mouth in a weak smile. "You mean Laurie. *She* ain't my missus. She's my girlchild. Laurie."

Brian grinned. He felt relieved, downright happy to hear that. Watching the girl approaching, he said, "She rides real good."

"One of the best. Damned fine ranch hand." Pride gleamed in Pearson's eyes. "We mean to send her East to school next winter. Make a damned fine lady out of her, too."

She galloped up and jerked rein. Squatting the bay on its haunches, she flung herself from the saddle and thrust the bandana full of snow at Brian. It was starting to melt and dripping at the bottom. He pulled away the bandana. Holding the snowball in one hand, he used the wet cloth to wipe lightly at the blood around Pearson's wound.

Despite himself, Pearson groaned at the touch.

Gently Brian covered the open gash with the bandana, then crushed the snow onto it. Pearson winced once. His body taut, his hands and face knotted, he lay still as Brian packed the snow against the wound.

The chill of the ice worked to stop the bleeding and numb the pain. Some of the tension eased out of Pearson's body. For a moment, his eyes had been pressed shut. He opened them to look at Brian. Catching a shallow breath, he said, "It's feeling better already."

"It'll help for a while," Brian told him. "But it'll hurt like hell when the snow's all melted."

Pearson knew as much.

"We've got to get him home," Laurie said to Brian. "We've got to get the doctor to him."

He nodded in agreement. "Either of your horses tame enough to haul a travvy?"

"They're not broke to drive. The bay's still green. You saw him try to kink up. Zeb's well broke but he's rump shy. He kicks. I don't know . . ." Her voice faded. She shook her head helplessly.

"We can use my horse," he suggested. "Old Red don't drive to harness, but he's too tired to raise much of a ruckus over anything. You wait here. I'll go cut poles."

As he rose to mount up, she flashed a small smile at him. Her teeth were even and white. Her lips were full and inviting. Her dark eyes held lively sparks.

Riding toward the forest, Brian wondered what kind of woman this girl in britches might be. In all his drifting, he had never run onto the like of her before.

CHAPTER
TWO

The nearest likely stand of timber was well uprange. As he neared it, Brian scanned the trees, hunting saplings suitable for travois poles. The breeze was coming to him from the forest. It brought him the dank green scents of the woods, the odors of rotting leaf mold, of wild animals and cattle. And of something not long dead.

A cowman tended to be curious why an animal died on his range. He wanted to know whether it went down to hunger or exposure or an accident, or maybe had been jumped by a painter-cat, or had drunk bad water, or been killed by disease. To keep his cattle alive and healthy, he needed to know what killed animals on his range.

Sam Pearson would want to know about it if there was a dead beef here. And Brian was too much a cowman not to be curious himself. From the smell, the carcass was close by. Investigating it wouldn't take him out of his way. He rode on into the trees.

He found the carcass lying in a shallow hollow. It was on its side, legs sticking out stiffly. The coyotes had ripped open the belly and gorged themselves. Buzzards had worked on the remains. But there was enough left for him to see this wasn't plain range beef. This had been a young bull, apparently a prime Durham stud.

If the bull wore a brand, it was lying on the marked side. The torn remnants of hide that were turned upward showed no traces of brand burns. Dismounting, Brian waved away the flies that swarmed around the decaying head. Breath held, he bent to look for earmarks. The ears were intact, the marks clear. Swallowtails, right and left.

And there was a bullet hole in the skull.

Backing off to draw breath, he muttered a curse. The swallowfork notches were Pearson's mark. Pearson's luck was running bad. Losing a fine bull like that would probably hurt a cowman like Pearson almost as much as the goring.

He glanced over the carcass, wondering why it had been shot. None of the legs were broken. The bones all seemed sound. He could spot no telltales of disease, and anyway a diseased carcass should have been buried or burned. But the bull had definitely been shot on purpose.

There was sign on the ground. A shod horse had stood by restlessly. Other horses, unshod, had grouped around. Their tracks were over the marks of iron. That was downright curious.

From the state of the carcass, it had happened a couple of days earlier. Maybe it was Pearson himself who shot the bull. If not, whoever had done it had probably reported it to Pearson already.

And right now, Sam Pearson was waiting with one hell of a bellyache. Turning away from the carcass, Brian hunted saplings for the travois.

When he got back with them, Laurie was at her father's side. She had taken time to tie the bay, but the dun was still leaning on the rope, holding the steer helpless on the ground.

Laurie rose to meet Brian. As he stepped down from his horse, he asked her, "How is he?"

"It's hurting him," she said. "He won't admit it, but it's hurting him."

Brian nodded, understanding. There was no way to stop the pain. "We'll get him home quick as we can. He'll rest easier there."

He lashed the poles into a framework and slung it from his saddle. He used the tarp from his bedroll to stretch between the drags, and one soogan to pad it. Then, as gently as they could, he and Laurie worked Pearson onto the travois. By the time they had finished covering him with Brian's other soogan and tying him in place, Pearson looked really bad. His face had faded to a very sickly gray. The sweat of pain and effort drenched him. Although his eyes were still open, they were glassy and unfocused, as if they saw nothing.

Laurie wiped tenderly at his face with her bandana. "Are you all right, Pa?"

He made a faint noise in his throat. His eyes just kept staring.

Brian didn't like the look of it. But he kept his voice calm and reassuring as he told her, "I don't think he heard you."

"He's not dying!"

"No, ma'am. I'd say he's just sort of passed out. It's best this way. He won't feel the pain so much while we're moving him."

She nodded in acceptance of what he said. Starting for the dun, she muttered, "I'll get my horse."

"Hold on, ma'am. I'll fetch him."

"I can get my own horse."

"Ma'am, that steer's lying there gathering its strength. Could be it'll come up snuffy. It wouldn't do us any good if it hooked you now."

"Or you!"

He could almost have grinned at the dogbone determined streak of independence in her. "Ma'am, I don't know the way to your place. I'd have a hard time getting your Pa home without you to show me the way. But I reckon you could handle the job now well enough without me."

"You know cows?" she asked, reluctant to give in but seeing the logic of his argument.

"I've tailed up a few," he told her.

The steer looked docile enough lying there at the end of the rope. He didn't trust it one damned bit. He glanced around for a rock. Spotting one that looked good, he scooped it up and tested its heft.

As he approached it, the steer rolled a white-rimmed eye at him. There was foam around its mouth and nostrils. And blood on one horn. He felt his gut knot at the thought of that horn ripping into his own belly.

He saw the steer tense, and he knew it would like to hook him just as it had Pearson. But the dun held the rope tight. Staying well clear of the rope, he stepped to the steer's head. He gauged the blow carefully. He didn't want to crack open the steer's skull, just knock the fight out of it. Aiming precisely, he swung. As the rock hit, the steer flinched. Its hoofs flailed.

That damned skull was harder than iron, Brian thought as he struck again. This time the steer went limp. It was stunned, but he didn't think it was out cold. Not for long. Grabbing slack from the dun, he recovered the loop quickly and jumped back.

By the time the steer realized it was no longer roped down, Brian had reached the horse and caught the nigh stirrup. He swung into the saddle as the steer got itself up off the ground.

The steer stood splay-legged, swaying its big head, looking groggy. Keeping the dun facing it, Brian brought in the throw rope. With the rope coiled and a loop set for use, he gigged the dun toward the steer.

Warily, the steer backstepped: a man on a horse was an altogether different matter from a man afoot. It gazed at Brian as he got between it and the bog. In position, blocking the steer from the mudhole and from Laurie and her father, Brian gave a hoot and waved the coiled rope. The steer wheeled. It broke into a staggering lope. Tail high, it headed for the distant timber.

Satisfied that it was no more threat, Brian returned to Laurie. She was already astride the bay, riding to meet him.

"Ma'am," he said as he came up to her, "my horse is too fagged out to ride and haul both. I'd be obliged to borrow the loan of a mount?" His question was only custom. He knew he would be welcome to the use of the dun. But a man didn't just help himself to another person's horse and saddle without leave.

"Of course," she said. "Look, I've been thinking. We'll have to keep that travvy moving along slow if we don't want to shake Pa up and hurt him worse."

He nodded agreement.

"And we need to get the doctor to him as quick as we can. Suppose I ride on ahead? Can you just follow my tracks? It's only about three miles to the house. You'd be on a trial before long."

"Yes, ma'am."

"Then I'll go on ahead. I'll tell Ma. I expect I'll have a fresh mount and be on my way for the doctor by the time you get to the house."

"Yes, ma'am," he said again, a little sad at losing her company. But she was right.

She shaped a smile for him. "Thank you, Mister — ?"

"Brian. Just Brian. No *mister* attached."

"Thank you, Brian. I hope I'll see you again." With that, she was riding on.

Brian collected the roan with the travois and set out behind her. She was moving at a fast-traveling trot. In a few minutes, she was out of his sight behind a piece of woods. He wondered if he would ever see her again.

Her tracks led him to the trail she had spoken of. It followed a small stream, winding through woods and around outcrops of rock. The trail was rough, the travel slow and wearisome. He felt as if he had covered well over three miles. At last, topping a ridge, he saw the ranch.

The basin ahead of him held a broad meadow surrounded by a ring of ridges. The cabin was off to his left. It sat on a slope, high enough to be well clear of winter drifts and of spring mud in the bottoms. Built of roughhewn logs, it looked small and squatty, though he judged the roof high enough to allow a loft. Glass-paned windows flanked the door. The heavy shutters were latched open. Through the glass, he could see the bright calico of curtains.

The cabin had no gallery, only a small stoop between the steps and the door. A woman was standing on the stoop, shading her eyes with one hand as she peered toward the ridge. A lop-eared hound sat beside her.

There had been a good big barn a ways from the cabin. Now there was only a smoke-stained stone foundation and a heap of charred rubble. A makeshift lean-to stood against a small shed nearby, sheltering a handy-wagon. Pole corrals held a few using horses. A bone-hipped, slack-mouthed old gray, apparently pensioned off, grazed loose in the cabin yard. At a respectable distance, a milk cow with a spring calf browsed new growth on some scrubby brush.

Scanning the basin, Brian saw a rider. Laurie. She was on the far slope. Even as he glimpsed her, she topped it and disappeared.

The hound spotted him as he rode through the gap and started down into the basin. It rose to head for him, tail at wary half cock. The woman called it back. Reluctantly, it returned to sit at her side. As Brian

19

neared, she gathered her skirts and hurried down from the stoop to meet him.

"How bad is it?" she called.

"Bad enough, I reckon," he said. Reaching her, he reined up. "It could be a lot worse."

She dashed past him to the travois.

It was poor custom for a man to step down from his saddle without an invite, but this time the circumstances were unusual. The woman had more important matters on her mind than manners. And Brian was bone weary. He took the liberty of sliding off his horse. Walking stiffly, he led the dun to the hitchrail in front of the cabin. The hound approached him, sniffing cautiously. He spoke to it as he tied the horse.

Returning to the woman, he asked, "Missus Pearson?"

She nodded in reply.

She looked about the same age as her husband. She was a tall woman. Taller than her man, Brian thought. She had a lean, rawboned look about her. Her hands were hard and slender. As she brushed a stray lock of yellow hair away from her face, he noticed she was missing half a little finger. Like a dally roper. He wondered how she had lost it.

"You're Mister Brian?" She had a faint trace of an accent. A little like the German folk from New Braunfels, he thought, but as she went on he decided it wasn't the same at all. She said, "Laurie told me what happened. She's gone for the doctor. Could you help me with him, please?"

"Yes, ma'am."

Pearson's face was still gray, with a sagging hollow look to it. The woman touched his cheek tenderly. His eyelids fluttered. They lifted slightly. Hoarsely, he said, "Hildy?"

"It's all right, Sam. You're home now." She turned to Brian. "Can we get him inside onto the bed?"

Brian nodded. He supposed he could manage Pearson in his arms, but he didn't think it would do the wound any good. Pearson shouldn't be joggled any more than necessary. Frowning thoughtfully, he studied the spread of the travois poles on the ground, then the door of the cabin. It was a good wide door. "I think we can haul the whole travvy inside with him on it, like a litter."

Pearson worked up enough voice to say, "I can walk in."

"Like hell you can," Brian answered him. "You want to jog your guts out that hole in your belly? You lie still. We'll fetch you in."

"I can walk in," Pearson mumbled. But there wasn't much strength to his protest.

"You shush up, Sam," Hildy told him. Her voice was gentle and loving in its chiding. "Mister Brian is a guest here. You be polite and pay some respect to what he's got to say."

Working together, Brian and Hildy unhitched the travois and lowered it to the ground. Brian tied the roan to the hitchrail, then stepped between the ends of the travois poles. Hildy took her place at the other end of the travois. Gripping the poles, Brian started slowly

21

to lift the makeshift litter. Hildy put her back to the job. She staggered a bit, but she managed. Together, they walked the litter to the steps and up into the cabin.

Inside, a wall divided the cabin into two rooms. The door between them stood open. Hildy nodded toward it. Brian swung around, hauling the litter on into a bedroom. The bed was a big brass-framed one, with a stack of featherbeds on it. They eased the litter down onto the featherbeds.

As Brian paused to peel his hat and coat and catch his breath, he asked, "The doctor is two days' ride? Two days going and two days coming back?"

"Yes. But he could get here quicker than that. Laurie is heading for the Bailey place. She'll be there by nightfall. I expect the Baileys will spell her. Send one of their boys on from there for us. If they do, he can ride all night. Be at the doctor's come morning. If the doctor is to home, he can come back to Bailey's and get a fresh mount and be here sometime the day after."

Pearson mumbled, "Don't need no doctor. Time he gets here, I'll be healed and forking broncs."

"You just don't want to pay him for the patching," Hildy scolded.

Pearson managed a feeble grin at her teasing.

"Ma'am, you handy at fixing hurts like this?" Brian asked her.

"I've been married to a working cowhand for twenty-two years," she replied.

"Then I reckon you can keep the wound tended proper until the doc gets here?"

"I expect so. I'd best set some water to boil and get it cleaned up. Mister Brian, could you strip him, make him as comfortable as you can?"

"Yes, ma'am. Glad to."

She hurried off to the other room. Brian unburdened himself of his gunbelt and chaps. Then he began to take the travois apart from under Pearson a pole at a time. When he finished that, he set to stripping Pearson out of his clothes.

Being home in his own bed with his wife close at hand seemed to be doing Pearson good. There was some color in his face. His eyes focused on Brian. He even tried to grin a bit as he worked up voice enough to make talk.

"Careful there," he said to Brian. "Don't you cut or tear nothing so it can't be mended again. I only just bought these britches a couple of years ago. Hildy'll give me breakfast on a shovel if I get them ruined this quick."

"They'll come off better than you do, and heal a damn sight quicker," Brian answered. "It's the longhandles I'm worried about. I expect they'll never fork a saddle again."

"Hell! Me and them longhandles have rode the range a long while together. I always figured we'd go on pardners until we both crossed over. Figured we'd be together when we ride them Golden Trails Up Yonder that the preachers are always talking about."

"Where a Texican goes when he dies, he don't need no longhandles." Brian decided the underwear would have to be cut off. "If you got some scissors around here, I'll put them out their misery quick."

"Top drawer." Pearson darted his eyes toward the tall dresser in the corner.

Brian found the scissors among spools of thread and balls of yarn. Returning to the bedside, he snipped at the longhandles.

"One damned thing after another," Pearson muttered. "First the barn, then the bull, and now this. Mister, I ain't up to much shouting. Will you give a holler for me, ask my missus if she's heard from the boys yet?"

Brian called over his shoulder at the open door, "Ma'am, you hear anything from the boys yet?"

"Not yet!" she shouted back.

"You got hired hands working for you?" Brian asked Pearson as he tugged away slashed pieces of underwear.

"Not hired ones. Just my sons. You reckon I'll be laid up long?"

"At least a couple of months, I'd guess. All depends."

"Hell," Pearson groaned.

He looked about to start brooding. To keep his mind off his troubles, Brian asked him, "Your boys good cowhands?"

"Damned good for the size of them. Jump, that's Sam Junior, he's fifteen. Near to sixteen now. Growing good. Eddie ain't but twelve. Smart as a whip and rides like a wild Indian, but he's light yet for the work."

Talking about his kids seemed to perk Pearson up. Brian said, "Your girl looks to be handy with a horse."

24

"For a female, she's a hell of a fine cowhand. But she's light, too. It ain't easy work for a woman. My Hildy there, she's a fine rider. She can herd with a man. Can't set a loop worth a damn though. I reckon you got to be born to it —" Pearson's voice suddenly caught in his throat as Brian pulled flannel away from the wound. Taking a shallow breath, he went on, "Texicans got it in their blood. Hildy, she's a Swede. Her old man pushed a plow. It worried me some that the boys might take after her side of the family. But they're turning out all Texican right down to the bootheels." He ran out of breath, his voice fading with a shudder.

"You gonna be all right?" Brian asked.

"Uh-huh. I've hurt worse," Pearson said through clenched teeth.

Brian cleared away the last shreds of the longhandles, then pulled up a quilt to cover Pearson.

"Mister Brian," Pearson said, "I'd be obliged if you'd tend my horse for me."

"I'd be obliged to throw mine in with yours for a feed," Brian said. "He's been rode a fair piece on short rations the past few days."

"Help yourself. Just help yourself to a fresh horse out of the corrals if you want. Any horse out there." Pearson eyed him. "You know, you look a mite gaunted yourself. Likely wouldn't hurt you or your horse to rest here awhile, if you ain't in a hurry."

"From the smell of your missus's vittles, it'd be a real pleasure," Brian drawled, thinking he'd like to stay around for at least four days. He allowed to himself he had a strong hankering to see Laurie again.

CHAPTER
THREE

The hound was sitting on the stoop when Brian came out of the cabin. It eyed him uncertainly. He held out his hand. The hound sniffed, gave his fingers a tentative lick, then offered him a wag of its tail. He patted its head and let it smell his hand again, wanting to be sure it would know him and his scent. Then he collected the horses and headed for the shed. The hound followed at his side.

The wind was changing. Sharp gusts brought a chill edge of dampness to him. He could see a gray haze shaping up in the north. There would be rain or snow by nightfall. He wondered about Laurie and whether she would reach the shelter of the Bailey place before the weather turned.

At the door of the shed, he stripped the saddle from the dun and examined its back. The ride up to Pearson's had been slow. The horse was dry and cool. Its back was clean of galls. He slung the saddle into the shed, then stripped the roan. It hadn't fared so well. His blanket was good and when he started out from Tallow Dip on the other side of Ade's Ridge, the saddle had been a good fit. But hard riding and short rations had gaunted the roan, sharpening its backbone. Long hours astride had forced Brian to shift around in the saddle, easing his legs. That was hard on a horse. The setfasts had started days ago. Now they looked raw and ugly. He hoped Pearson had some white-oak bark he could boil down to poultice the sores.

Holding a tight cheek, he lifted the roan's nigh fore hoof. The horn was growing too long. The nails were beginning to ream out the holes. One nail was gone. The shoe was almost worn through at the toe. The other fore hoof was about as bad. He didn't try to examine the hind hoofs. The roan wouldn't stand for it without a leg tied up, and he was too tired to bother with that now. He supposed the back was as bad as the front. He would have to pull the shoes all around and rasp down the hoofhorn. Renew the shoes, too, if Pearson could spare him the iron.

When he had watered the horses, he turned them into a corral. He waited, watching, until both had rolled. Then he went to the shed for feed. The hound followed along. It waited outside as he went in. He found the grain in a tinlined bin. There were morrals hanging from nails above the bin. Just as he started to scoop grain into one, he heard the hound growl. The sound was ominous. Dropping the morral, he stepped to the door.

The hound was sniffing the wind, gazing at the north ridge. Brian saw riders coming over the ridge. His hand went instinctively to his thigh. But the gun that should have been holstered there was back in Pearson's room.

There were four riders, young men wrapped in trade blankets, striding shaggy, bone-hipped ponies. Each carried a rifle across his mount's withers. Cheyenne, Brian thought, and a ways off the reservation. They looked more like hunters than a war party. Still, he wished to hell his gun wasn't so far away.

The lean-to blocked his view of the cabin from the shed. Nothing blocked the Indians' view of the shed. If he bolted for the cabin, he would be an easy target.

But maybe they didn't mean trouble.

Maybe.

He wondered if Hildy would see them and do something to protect herself. He was afraid she might be too concerned with her injured husband to notice what was happening in the yard.

Cautiously, he stepped out of the shed. Far enough to show himself to the Indians. Not so far that he couldn't lunge back to cover if need be.

The hound had its hackles up, and the growling continued in its chest. It rubbed against his leg, looking to him for orders.

"Steady, boy," he said quietly. He put a hand on its head. The growling stopped. The dog sat. Brian spread his hands then to show the oncoming Indians that they were empty.

The riders stopped well across the yard from him. They exchanged words with each other. Three stood waiting. The fourth came on at a walk. He rode up to the shed warily, his rifle held without threat but ready enough to be brought up and used.

He was a lean man with a pockmarked face. His eyes were hollow and tired and far too old-looking for the rest of his face. He'd had a hard winter, Brian thought.

Halting a couple of paces away, the Indian looked Brian over.

"Howdy," Brian said.

The Indian studied him a moment longer. Moving his pony a stride closer, he gestured and asked, "Where Pearson?"

Brian didn't want to admit that Pearson was laid up helpless. He didn't want to lie either. He said, "He ain't right here right this minute."

He spoke slowly, shaping each word carefully, hoping this Indian knew enough of the language to understand him. He had some Kiowa and some Comanche and a piece more sign talk, but he hadn't had many dealings with the Cheyenne before. He didn't want to make any mistakes. Plain ignorance could get a man into a lot of trouble with Indians. He felt naked as hell without a gun.

The Indian considered him, then said, "Friend?"

He wasn't sure whether the Indian was asking if he was Pearson's friend, or offering to be a friend. He pointed to himself, then to the Indian. "Friend."

The Cheyenne made no response. So Brian reckoned he was asking about Pearson. Pointing at himself, then in the direction of the cabin, he said, "Friends. Me and Pearson friends."

The Indian glanced at the hound skulking at Brian's side as if the dog could confirm Brian's claim. Then he gestured at himself. "Bent Knee. You make talk Pearson, say Bent Knee come go take eat beef."

His hands moved as he spoke, indicating Brian, the cabin, the ridges, the fact of a cow, and of eating.

Brian said, "You want me to tell Pearson that Bent Knee came and took a beef to eat?"

Bent Knee held up a hand, showing Brian four fingers. He pointed at himself, then at each of his companions. "Come go take beef. One, two, three, four."

"You want me to tell Pearson you took four head of beef?"

Bent Knee nodded.

Brian wasn't sure how Pearson would take to the idea. Cautiously, he suggested, "Four's a lot of cows. Too many."

Again, Bent Knee counted off himself and his companions. "One. Two. Three. Four."

He looked at Brian and added, "Him-woman ride run come go one. Him-woman good hair. Pretty hair." His hands made the signs of a woman on a horse, riding fast, alone. A gesture of hair. A scalp.

Brian got the drift. The Indians had seen Laurie riding off to the Bailey place all alone. Bent Knee was suggesting it would have been easy for him and his friends to lift her scalp.

He swallowed at his rising anger. It wouldn't do him any good to get mad. Especially when he didn't have a gun at hand. With a solemn shake of his head, he said, "If anything was to happen to her, the soldiers would come. You know soldiers? Many guns. Many soldiers. Too many. Very bad for Indians." His hands indicated riders. Battle. Dead men.

Bent Knee understood him well enough, and wasn't at all happy with what he was saying. Bent Knee wanted no war. He gazed at Brian with a kind of sad defiance. "Soldiers come, much die. Much bad. Much hurt Indian woman, Indian young. Indians fight. Much hurt white men. Much kill. Much hurt white men. Soldiers much bad."

Brian nodded, agreeing that war would hurt them all.

Bent Knee swung an arm, indicating the whole range. "Ago time, much grass. Much meat. Indians eat meat. Beef come go eat grass. White men eat meat. Much beef. Beef eat grass. No meat for Indian. Indian come go take eat beef."

It made sense. Before the cattle came there had been plenty of game on the range and the Indians could eat their fill of it. Then the white men started taking the game. Now the cattle ate the grass and the game was scarce, and the Indians couldn't understand why they shouldn't eat the beef.

Gesturing toward the cabin, then the range and then at himself, Bent Knee said, "Pearson much friend. Him-woman much friend. Bent Knee much friend. All much friend. Much beef. Bent Knee come go take eat one, two, three, four beef. Pearson come go take much beef." He opened and closed his fingers, indicating that Pearson could take more cattle than could be counted. "No soldiers."

He sounded like he meant Pearson had given him beef before without bringing the soldiers into it. He looked sad. Weary and winter-worn.

After his own long hungry ride through the icy ridges, Brian could sympathize with the Indians. He

31

thought of the calf he had killed to fill his own belly. Likely the Indians would take cattle whether they had permission or not. They were just being decent about it, asking first.

"All right," he said slowly, well aware he hadn't the right to give Pearson's cattle away. He figured he could square it somehow with Pearson. But he could be in a hell of a lot of trouble if he gave away any of those other brands out on the range. "But mind you only take Forked P beef. Savvy?" He traced the shape of the brand in the air with his finger. "Only Forked P."

"Forked P," Bent Knee said with a nod. He seemed to know about brands. Touching heels to his pony's flanks, he turned back to his companions.

Brian stood watching until the Indians were out of sight. As they disappeared over the ridge, he became aware of the knot in his chest. His palms were sweaty. He wiped them down his pants leg. As the wind touched him, he shivered. The hound rubbed against his leg, whining. He patted its head to reassure it. From now on, he told himself, he didn't step out of the house without his gun.

Once he was certain the Indians were well away, he finished feeding the horses, then returned to the cabin.

Hildy was in the bedroom with her husband. She had moved Brian's gear off the chair and drawn it up next to the bed. She sat at Pearson's side with one of his hands in hers.

"Mister Brian?" she called as she heard the door open.

32

Going to the bedroom door, he told her, "Just Brian, ma'am. No need for that *mister.*"

She smiled at him.

Pearson was covered to the neck with quilts, only his face and one hand showing. He lay still, looking at rest. And looking a lot better than he had earlier. His voice wasn't so tight with pain now as he asked, "Horses all right?"

"Uh-huh." With his hat in his hands, Brian went to the bedside. "I got a message for you. From an Indian name of Bent Knee."

"Bent Knee? Was he here?" Pearson sounded like he knew the Indian all right.

Brian nodded. "He said he'd come for some cows."

"Cows? More than one?"

"Four." Brian held up four fingers, the way Bent Knee had done.

"Hell! He must be feeding the whole damned nation!"

"Now, Sam," Hildy said soothingly, giving Pearson's hand a gentle squeeze.

"He's out to ruin me!" Pearson groaned. "He'll bleed me dry! He'll strip my range!"

"I tried to augur him some," Brian said apologetically, thinking he had hardly argued at all. He glanced around for his gear. It was hanging from a wall peg, the gunbelt on top. He reached for it. "I reckon I didn't augur him enough. Maybe I can catch up and tell him different."

"Hold on a minute, boy." Pearson started to sit up. A jolt of pain stopped him. He sunk back onto his pillow, sucking aching breaths.

"Shush up, Sam," Hildy said to him. She turned to Brian. "Sam's all bark and no bite. He'll holler about Bent Knee and those Cheyenne, but he'd have done the same. He's as kindly toward Bent Knee's people as if they was kinfolk. He'd let them take every beef on the range if they was to ask."

Brian had started to buckle the belt around his waist. He paused, looking at her in question.

Pearson spoke up for himself. "You ever eat buffalo, Brian?"

"Plenty."

"Kill them yourself?"

"Sometimes."

"The buffalo belong to the Indians, same as the beef belongs to us."

Hildy nodded, agreeing with her husband. She said, "Before the white man came to this country, the Indians had plenty of buffalo. Plenty of land. Everything that walked on the land was theirs. Now we've got the land and we've taken the buffalo, and the Indians are on hard times while our beef gets fat on the grass. There's been times all Sam and the children and me had to eat was buffalo. Now the Indians need meat and we've got beef. We can spare them a few head." She squeezed her husband's hand again. "Can't we, Sam?"

"Yeah," Pearson mumbled. "But the way things are going, it's gonna be a hard year for us, too."

"Brian, you just forget about Bent Knee," Hildy said. Her eyes indicated the gunbelt, suggesting he hang it up again. "There's coffee cooking. It should be ready by now. If you'd care for a cup, you just help yourself."

"Obliged." Brian returned the gunbelt to the peg, dropped his hat over it, and went on into the other room.

The coffee was ready. He found himself a cup and poured it full, then settled at the table. Overhead, the cabin creaked as the winds from the north blew cold. Be dark before long, and he wondered again about Laurie.

After a while, Hildy came from the bedroom. She pulled the door almost closed behind her, and said softly to Brian, "He's sleeping now."

"It'll do him good." He matched his tone to hers.

"He's been hurt before." She went to the fireplace and lifted the lid on the Dutch oven. The aroma of roasting venison gusted out. She poked the meat with a fork. "He's always got well again."

"Likely he will this time, too," Brian said. "I've seen men hurt worse and get over it, good as new again."

Replacing the lid, she darted a smile at him. "He will. He's a strong man."

She poured coffee for herself and sat down across the table from Brian. "We got married back in Texas just before the war, Sam and me. Soon as Texas joined the Confederacy, he went off to fight. He got wounded bad then, but he got over it. He'll be all right."

"Yes, ma'am."

She needed to talk to ease her tensions. She went on. "We knew some hard times back in Texas. We didn't have much then. By the time the war was over, nobody in Texas had much. The carpetbaggers and scalawags cleaned out what was left."

Brian nodded. He didn't remember the war times, but he had heard stories about them. And he knew the hard times that had still been in Texas long after the war.

"Wasn't much at all except wild cows in the brush," Hildy said. "So Sam went into the cattle business. A man could drop his loop on anything that didn't wear a brand in those days. The cattle were free for the taking. The work was in getting them to a market. Sam did it. He worked hard for us. We built up a nice little spread. Then the panic of seventy-three came along and we lost it all."

"You got a nice place here," Brian commented.

She nodded. "We worked for it. All of us. Believe me, we worked. There was free land here, and some Texas folk had come up ahead of us, and we knew they were getting along, so we loaded everything we had and left Texas. We came here with five half-broke cayuses and a couple of dozen head of mavericks hardly fit to make the walk, and just what goods we could pack on one old wagon. We didn't need but the one wagon to hold all we had. Just as well. The wagon kept breaking down. We had us a time rolling it this far. But we kept going and we got here."

She sounded wistful and sad, but proud at the same time. "We got here and we stayed and we built us a herd and a house and we mean to stay here. We'll hold on and stay set and no barn fires or wild steers or anything else will stop us!"

From the iron in her voice, Brian thought likely she was right. If her husband could survive that injury, they'd pull through.

She dropped her gaze from his face to his hands. She studied them as if she were reading sign in them. He glanced at them himself. There was sign to be read. The knuckles were hard, the fingers callused. The skin was weathered and scarred. They were hands marked by leather and iron, by the thorny brasada and the grass ropes, and even occasionally by pick handles and saloon brawls.

When she looked into his face again, she asked, "Were you sent to us, Brian?"

"Ma'am?"

"Did someone tell you that you could find work with us?"

"No, ma'am. I was just drifting through when I ran into your husband and girl."

"You are a cowhand by trade, aren't you?"

He had tried other lines that he had hoped would make him more money quicker and easier, but he always seemed to end up chousing beef. Nodding, he said, "I reckon I've dropped a few loops and burnt a few hides."

She glanced at his hands again. "You've been working in the brush country."

"Yes, ma'am."

"Ever work hill country like this?"

"I reckon I've worked near about every kind of country there is. I worked a place up to the north of here that was so high the cows fell off the range into eagle nests."

She smiled slightly. "Looking for work now?"

"I'd better be. I've scraped the bottom out of my poke and lost most of my pawn up in the snows."

"I don't know," she muttered, as if she were speaking to herself. Then she said, "The past few years, since we got a decent herd built up, we always hired a man on in the spring to help Sam through the season. This year we figured we could squeeze by on our own. Jump is getting big enough to carry his own weight. Laurie and Eddie are a lot of help. If need be, I can ride roundup myself. I can work." She held up her hand, showing him the stump of the damaged finger. "I lost that to a wild horse I was helping Sam take. Bit it clean off. Kicked me, too, and busted three ribs."

He gave a sympathetic shake of his head. She was quite a woman. He wondered if Laurie would shape up into the same kind.

"That didn't stop us. We got him. Made a fine roping horse out of him. More coffee?"

"Obliged."

She refilled his cup, then her own. After taking a sip, she told him, "Thing is, we figured Sam and Jump could handle the cow work. Eddie could take over the wrangling Jump was doing. We thought we wouldn't have to pay out a wage for a hired man. We borrowed money and invested in upgrading our beef. We were planning on enough profit to pay that back and to send Laurie off East to school come winter. Now with all this . . ." Her voice faded into a sigh.

Then she went on, "Now, even if we don't send Laurie off to school, we've still got our debts to pay. I just can't see any way we can promise a man a foreman's wage. What we need now is a foreman. A top hand who can take over and run this place. Somebody who can handle our share of the roundup and the branding and the drive, and see us through. The best we can afford is a plain old forty-and-found hired hand. It'll skin us close just to pay that. You understand me, Brian?"

He nodded, but he said, "I ain't the man you want, ma'am."

"I know forty and found isn't much to offer for the job that needs doing. But next year — Brian, I know Sam won't ever be as good as new again. I was talking to him about it a while ago. We figure we'll have to have a man on steady here. Even when Jump's full grown. By then we hope the place will be big enough to need a whole crew. You stay with us, Brian. See us through this season. You'll eat decent and have some spending money, and a place to winter. And next year, once the debts are paid, we'll give you a share in the profit. You see us through and a piece of this ranch will be yours."

He gave a slow shake of his head. Not quite meeting her eyes, he said, "I ain't the man you want. I ain't the kind for it. I ain't much for staying put from one year to the next. I'm a drifter."

"You mean you don't want the responsibility," she said.

He started to protest. But he realized she was right. He didn't want to be tied down with responsibility, or owing to anyone. He didn't want people depending on him. He was willing to work a season as a common cowhand to fill his poke for the winter. He wanted nothing more than that, except maybe quick wealth.

"Brian, you're a cowhand," Hildy was saying. "From the look of you, you know the work. You seem like a smart man. I'm sure you can do the job. I think Providence sent you to us."

He flashed an embarrassed grin at her. "No, ma'am, it wasn't Providence. It was restlessness. I went up to Tallow Dip last year hoping to get hold of some of that quick money the miners are taking out of the ground there. I got snowed in and stuck there all winter. I wouldn't have come out in this direction at all, but I heard the trail through Tinker's Pass over Ade's Ridge had opened up, and I was too damned restless to wait for the wagon road down the other side to thaw out. I set off through the pass and almost got buried in an avalanche and damned near lost in the late snows. That's how I come here when I did."

"And you claim that's not the work of Providence?"

He met her eyes and saw the certainty in them, and wondered if there was a chance she might be right. He didn't think so. He wasn't cut out to boss a spread. He didn't want responsibility. He sure as hell didn't want to own a piece of a ranch and stay set in one place for the rest of his life.

"You want to think about it, maybe sleep on the idea before you decide?" Hildy asked.

He gave a nod, even though he was sure he would say no come morning.

Suddenly solemn, she said, "There is one thing you should know before you decide. You're entitled to know the worst of it."

"Ma'am?"

"You saw that our barn burnt down?"

"Yes, ma'am."

"I don't believe that was any accident. I think somebody fired our barn. I've got no notion who in the world it might have been, but I've got a deep feeling there's going to be more trouble around here before the summer is out. If you do come in with us, you may be taking on a share in it."

"Ma'am," he said impulsively, "there's only two things that a Texican is scared of. One of them is being set afoot. The other one *ain't* trouble."

She smiled as if he had agreed to stay. He started to protest, to make it clear that he hadn't meant it that way. But a sound snatched his attention.

Maybe Hildy's talk of trouble had primed him, or maybe it was that visit from the Indians. Whatever, it made him want a gun in his hand. Glancing around, he saw a rifle racked near the door. He rose to take it down as he told Hildy, "Horses coming."

CHAPTER
FOUR

Rifle in hand, Brian opened the door. A gust of wind hit him in the face. A thin mist of snow rode the wind. He squinted against it, looking for the source of the sounds.

The hound heard the hoofbeats, too. It had been curled up under the stoop. Squeezing out, it sniffed the wind, then trotted off with its tail waving. It acted as if it scented a friend.

Two riders appeared, galloping toward the cabin. The hound hurried to meet them. Brian eased back, letting the rifle hang loosely in his hand.

Hildy had followed him to the door. She looked out over his shoulder. "That's Laurie!"

"So quick?" Brian grunted. "Who's that with her? Not the doctor?"

Hildy watched a hopeful moment more as the riders came closer. Slumping with disappointment, she said, "No, it's Frank Hunt."

"Who's he?"

"He owns a ranch here in the valley. South of us." She cocked a brow. "You reckon there's been more trouble?"

He hoped not. He didn't answer, but stepped back to return the rifle to its rack. Hildy took his place in the doorway.

The riders were coming in fast, with the dog running alongside. As they reined up, Laurie called to her mother, "I ran into Frank and Pike! Frank sent Pike to bring the doctor!"

Frank Hunt touched his hatbrim to Hildy, then stepped from his saddle. He offered Laurie a hand down. Accepting it, she slid from her horse almost into his arms. For a moment they stood together with Hunt half holding her. Then she turned to the cabin.

Hunt followed her. He was a tall man, standing a head higher than the girl. He closed the door behind him and pulled off his hat. His hair was dark, touched with traces of gray at the temples. Some gray threaded through his thick mustache. His face was lean but his shoulders were broad. He stood with the straight stiffness of a professional soldier, a schooled officer. He gave Brian the slight nod of one stranger to another, and gave Hildy a friendly smile. "Evening, ma'am."

"Evening, Frank," Hildy said with neighborly sociability. But undertones of tension haunted her voice. She gestured at Brian. "Frank, this is Mister Brian. Laurie told you about Sam?"

Hunt nodded.

"Brian helped her fetch him home when he got hurt."

Hunt's face shaped concern as he asked, "Is the injury serious?"

"It don't look good," Hildy admitted.

Hunt peeled his coat and dropped it onto a wall peg. Under it, he wore a holstered Colt revolver. He stripped the gunbelt and put it with the coat, as if he felt free to make himself at home in the Pearsons' house. He asked Hildy, "May I see him?"

"He's asleep now."

"Don't wake him just for me."

She nodded as if she'd had no intention of doing it.

Laurie hung up her own coat and hat, then went to the cupboard. She took down two cups and held one out in invitation. "Coffee, Frank?"

"Thank you." He smiled at her. Turning to Hildy, he said, "You'll need someone to take over the ranch work while Sam's laid up. I'll stay here until Pike gets back with the doctor. Then —"

"No need," Hildy interrupted. "We'll get along."

"You'll have to have a man around the place." Hunt wasn't asking. He was telling her.

With an edge of defiance in her voice, she said, "I've asked Brian to stay on."

Hunt looked at Brian. His eyes were narrow and critically appraising. "You're going to need someone you can *depend* on."

Laurie came up carrying the cups of coffee. She held one out to Hunt. Cocking a brow at him, she said in a teasing tone, "I think we can depend on Brian."

"Laurie, this is serious. Your father is badly injured and you need help. You need someone you know. Not some dragtail saddle tramp who's likely to drift off when the work starts getting hard."

Brian felt his hands tense, wanting to clench into fists. He might shun responsibility, but he had never in his life run out on a job just because it was hard work.

Hildy was looking hopefully at him. "You will stay, won't you, Brian?"

Impulsively, he nodded.

She smiled with relief.

Hunt said to her, "You're making a mistake."

"Why, Frank!" Laurie said with an air of teasing. "Do you know Mister Brian?"

Hunt gave a shake of his head. "I know his kind. I've tried hiring them on myself. I've always regretted it."

"What the hell you mean *my kind!*" Brian snapped at him.

Back stiff, head high, Hunt looked down his nose at Brian. It wasn't easy for him. Brian was as tall as he was. "An officer learns to read character. He learns quickly. There are times when his life may depend on his knowing and understanding the men under him. I know a fiddlefoot when I see one."

Laurie spoke to Brian. "Frank was in the Army. He was a captain." She sounded proud of the fact.

"Have you ever been in the Army?" Hunt said to Brian.

Brian shook his head. He had been far too young for the war between the states, and he had never been of a notion to go fighting Indians just for the hell of it. He replied, "I've always done my own fighting. Never needed a company of soldiers to back me up."

Hildy saw trouble building. Meaning to head it off, she stepped between the two men. "Frank, I'm obliged to you for your offer to help, but there just ain't any way I can accept. I can't impose on you. You've got your own place to run and your own work to do. You're going to be as busy as any of us getting ready for branding."

"Pike can handle things at my place," he answered. "I'll hire on a couple of men to help him. I'll take care of things here."

She shook her head insistently. "You've got your own place and your own work. We'll take care of ourselves."

A teasing smile played on Laurie's lips as she spoke to Hunt. "I'm sure Brian can take care of us just fine."

Hildy turned to her. "Laurie, you've got a sweated horse outside in the snow!"

Laurie had forgotten about that. She wheeled to set down her coffee and grab her coat. As she dashed out, Hunt snatched his own coat and hurried after her. "I'll give you a hand!"

Over her shoulder, Laurie called back to her mother, "We'd better put up Frank's horse, too, hadn't we? He is staying for supper, ain't he?"

"If he's willing," Hildy answered politely, but she didn't look pleased at the idea.

Once the door had closed behind Laurie and Hunt, Brian turned to Hildy. "They're right friendly, ain't they?"

"He wants to marry her," Hildy said. She stepped to the fireplace for a look at the roast in the Dutch oven.

"Only you don't like the idea?" he asked.

Her back was to him. She shrugged. "It's not exactly that. Truth is, Sam and me think she's too young yet to know her own mind. We've got nothing against Frank, only that he keeps pushing her and there's times she seems real close to accepting him."

"You could always speak out against it," he suggested. "You're her folks. She can't up and get married unless you agree to it."

"Uh-huh. But back when Sam and me were courting, my Pa said no to us. He wanted me to marry some good solid Swedish farmer, not a wild Texican like Sam. Me and Sam had to run away together. I had to lie about my age. We agreed then that we wouldn't ever make any young'un of ours do the same. We swore we'd let our young'uns make up their own minds. We can't go against that. But we'd a lot sooner Laurie waited awhile. She needs to meet more different fellers before she settles on one. She doesn't meet many men around here, except for cowhands who work the summer for a stake and then throw it all away living high in town through the winter. None of them are looking to settle down. We want to give her a chance to know more proper, decent young men before she gets herself promised to anybody."

"That's why you want to send her East to school?" he asked.

She nodded. Looking over her shoulder at him, she said, "Brian, I'd be obliged if you'd tend the stock in the corral for me. And if you see Laurie lollygagging out there, remind her there's a cow to be milked."

"Yes, ma'am." Remembering the Indians, he strapped on his gunbelt before he pulled on his coat. Setting his hat on his head, he stepped outside.

47

Laurie and Hunt had turned their horses into the corral and were standing in the lee of the feed shed. They stood very close to each other. Hunt's head bowed as he spoke to her. She laughed. The wind brought Brian the music of her laughter. Irked, he called out, "Miss Laurie, your ma says don't forget the milk cow!"

Hunt lifted his head to glare at Brian. Laurie tugged his sleeve. Together, they set off across the yard toward the cow and calf. Brian went on to the shed to fetch feed for the penned horses. While he was inside, he heard Hunt and Laurie lead the cow into the lean-to built against the shed. When he went out with the grain, he went around the far end of the shed avoiding them. He lingered at the corral until the horses had finished eating. By then, Laurie was done with the milking. She and Hunt had disappeared. He wondered if they were back in the cabin under Hildy's watchful eye, or were wandering outside with Hunt sweet-talking the girl. He had half a mind to nose around and find out. But, dammit, it was none of his business.

The snow clouds that thickened the sky were bringing an early dusk. Shoulders hunched against the chill wind, he started for the cabin. The hound was lying on the stoop, curled into a tight ball. As he neared, it lifted its head. He paused when he realized it was looking past him. Its cocked ears listened to some sound he hadn't caught.

Thinking of the Indians, he flipped back the skirt of his coat and wrapped his hand around the butt of his gun as he turned to look into the wind.

The sounds reached him. Hoofbeats. Two horses at a traveling trot. He spotted two riders topping a ridge. The hound saw them too. Its tail waved as it started out to meet them. So they were friends, Brian decided. Letting his hand fall away from the gun, he went on into the warmth of the cabin. He found Hildy alone in the living room.

"You got more company coming," he told her.

She went to the door. For a moment, she stood looking out. When she turned to Brian again, there was relief in her voice. "It's the boys."

"Your sons?"

She nodded.

He stripped his coat then and took off the gunbelt to hang it with the coat. He took note of the empty wall pegs. Neither Laurie's coat nor Hunt's coat hung there. So the two of them were still outside.

He could hear the oncoming horses shift from a trot to a lope as they entered the yard. The dog yapped happily, announcing their arrival. Standing in the doorway, Hildy called to the riders, "Boys! Come on in here a minute before you unsaddle!"

"Yes, ma'am," a young voice replied. Leather squealed and bit chains rattled as the boys dismounted and hitched their horses.

The first boy through the door was unmistakably Sam Pearson's son. His features proclaimed it. He was as tall as Sam, but he hadn't his father's flesh yet. He was gangly and loose-jointed, running to bone. His shoulders didn't fill the coat he wore. Likely in a year or two they would.

The boy who followed him was smaller and younger with the straw-colored hair and light eyes of his mother, but his father's nose and mouth. His pale eyes were wide with curiosity.

The older boy, Jump, asked, "What's wrong, Ma?"

Hildy put a quality of unruffled confidence into her voice as she told them, "There's been a kind of accident. Your pa's got hurt —"

Jump read past her forced calm. Apprehensively, he interrupted. "Bad?"

"It's not too bad," she said. "He's asleep now. We've sent for the doctor. There's nothing to fret about."

The younger boy, Eddie, accepted his mother's pose. Interested but unworried, he asked, "What happened to him?"

"He was gored," she said.

"Was it that old bull that hooked him?"

"A steer."

"Ma —" Jump began. He hesitated. Turning to Eddie with an air of authority, he said, "You'd best go tend to the horses."

Eddie didn't want to go. He made a moan of objection. But he obeyed the order. As he went out, he slammed the door behind him.

Jump spoke to his mother, his voice soft and confidential. "He can't hear now. You can tell me the truth about Pa." He sounded like he expected the worst.

"I told you the truth," Hildy said quietly. "It's not bad, and he's asleep now, and there's nothing to worry about."

50

"You sure?"

"Jump, would you call your own ma a liar?"

His face reddened. "No, only I just thought — Ma, I ain't a little kid any more. I'm old enough now that you don't have to keep things back from me."

"I'm not keeping anything back from you. When your Pa wakes up, you can talk to him yourself." She gestured toward the bedroom.

He glanced at the closed door, then nodded. Shrugging off his coat, he turned to put it on a peg. That was when he first noticed Brian. He halted sharply with a grunt of surprise.

Hildy said, "Brian, this here is our son, Jump. Jump, Mister Brian is going to be helping out here until your pa's up again."

Jump wheeled to face his mother. "Pa said we wouldn't be hiring help this year!"

"Things have changed. We've got to have somebody take your pa's place on roundup."

"My pa's place!" Jump protested. "No! *I'll* do it! I'm riding this year. I can handle the work!"

"Not alone, you can't. We have to have a man to take your pa's place," Hildy told him.

He scowled at Brian and gave a defiant shake of his head. "I'm not wrangling again this year! I'm riding as a cowhand! Eddie can wrangle!"

Hildy nodded. "Sure, Eddie can wrangle. We'll need more than one rider. You'll work with Mister Brian."

Jump eyed Brian as he considered. He knew his mother was right about the need for two riders. He said, "All right. I'll pick a string for him."

Brian caught the implication. Jump was willing to accept a hired hand under his orders, not a boss over him.

Hildy understood, too. She frowned. "Mister Brian can pick his own string. And yours."

"*I* know our horses!" Jump snapped. "*I* know our range. What does *he* know?"

"He knows the cow business," she answered firmly. "Jump, your pa is laid up and he'll be laid up for a while. Somebody has to step in and take over for him."

"*I* can do it!" he insisted.

"There ain't anything going to get done if everybody is pulling crossed reins," she said. "Son, it's been a long time since I figured you were too big to have your backside tanned, but you keep acting this way and you'll get bottomed like a baby. You hear?"

Angry embarrassment flushed Jump's face. He glared at his mother. She gazed back at him with steady determination.

The standoff was suddenly interrupted as the door slammed open. Eddie dashed in. Eagerly, he asked, "Can I see him, Ma? Can I see Pa?"

She turned from Jump to answer Eddie. "Not now. He's asleep. If you haven't wakened him charging in here like a wild bull."

"I'm sorry."

Hildy didn't want to go on arguing with Jump. She spoke to both boys. "Did you find the bull?"

"Not a hair of him," Eddie said.

Jump realized there was nothing to be gained from going on with the argument. But he wasn't going to give in. He turned his back on Brian. Sniffing the air, he said, "I smell coffee." His voice had a quality of command, as if he were ordering his mother to offer him a cup.

Hildy cocked a brow at him. Her tone was equally commanding. "You take your spurs off first."

He made no reply. For a moment he just stood in silent defiance of her. Then, wheeling away, he walked on past her. There was anger in his every movement as he tromped to the staircase at the back of the room. He climbed the stairs heavily, his bootheels slapping the treads and his spurs jangling.

Once he had disappeared into the loft, Hildy spoke to Brian. "I'm sorry about that."

"No harm, ma'am," Brian answered, wondering how the hell he was going to handle the ranch work with help like Jump.

"He'll cool down when he's had time to think things over. He'll see how it is. He's just awful young yet. Goes off half-cocked sometime. You'll have to sort of look out for him, Brian."

He nodded.

Eddie was looking from one to the other in bewilderment. In hope of some explanation, he said, "Ma?"

Hildy turned to him and introduced him to Brian, then said, "Eddie, ain't you learned yet to take your spurs off in the house?"

"Yes, ma'am." He pulled off the spurs and his chaps. As he was hanging them on a peg, he said, "Me and Jump rode halfway to yesterday looking for that old bull, only we didn't see no sign of him. Didn't Pa and Laurie turn up nothing?"

"I didn't think to ask," Hildy said.

Brian asked, "What bull is that, ma'am?"

"We got us a new he-animal." She beamed with pride. "A pure-blooded shorthorn. We figure to upgrade our stock with him. We had him in the barn but when it burnt he got loose and ran off. He's what everybody's been out looking for today. We'd like to fetch him back and keep him away from the cows until we've finished the branding."

Brian felt a sinking in his stomach. Reluctantly, he asked, "A Durham bull? Earmarked with swallowtails right and left?"

"That's him!" Eddie said. "Did you see him?"

Hildy asked, "Whereabouts?"

"Off not far from where your husband got hooked," Brian said. "Ma'am . . ."

His tone told her more than his words. Her smile disappeared. "Something's wrong? With the bull?"

"Yes, ma'am. He's dead."

"Oh no!" She wheeled away from Brian. Her shoulders went stiff. She stared at the bedroom door as if she looked through it at the injured man behind it. "Not the bull! Not now!"

Eddie faced Brian. "What do you mean, mister? Our bull ain't dead."

There was no way of changing facts. Brian said, "A Durham bull about four, five years old, earmarked with swallowforks is."

Hildy turned back to ask, "What happened to him?"

54

"He was shot. I figured you-all or one of your neighbors did it. I thought he must have been hurt or diseased or something."

"No. He was fine just three days ago, before the barn burnt."

"You reckon he got burnt in the fire before he run off?" Eddie suggested.

Jump had gotten himself in hand. He had stripped his chaps and spurs in the loft and was coming down again. From the steps, he called, "What? Who got burnt?"

"The bull!" Eddie told him. "Mister Brian says somebody shot our bull!"

Brian said, "It didn't look like he'd been burnt. From what I could see, he looked to be sound enough."

Jump glowered at Brian as if he thought Brian were lying to him. He demanded, "Who'd shoot our bull?"

"Somebody who come across him hurting somehow," Brian said. "A man puts a hurt animal out of its misery."

Hildy said, "If one of our neighbors did it, he'll be by to tell us about it."

"*He* said the bull was sound." Jump gave a nod at Brian. "None of our neighbors would kill our bull! Not if it was sound!"

"I said from what I could see it looked sound," Brian said.

Hildy suggested, "Maybe somebody ought to ride out tomorrow and have a look-see at the carcass."

"Yeah!" Jump agreed. "Maybe somebody shot our bull for some damned reason of his own!" His eyes accused Brian of having done it.

"Jump!" Hildy snapped. "You mind your language in this house!"

He glared at her defiantly. Unspeaking, he walked on down the steps and over to the fireplace. His back to her, and to Brian, he helped himself to a cup of coffee.

"Can I have some too?" Eddie asked hopefully.

Hildy hesitated as if she didn't approve of the younger boy drinking coffee.

"I've been riding hard and cold all day," Eddie pleaded. "I need it to warm my insides." He looked to Brian for understanding.

Brian nodded in agreement.

"All right," Hildy allowed. "Just one cup."

Eddie threw Brian a proud, pleased grin, then hurried to claim his cup of coffee.

Hildy looked at Brian. Her face was weary. Her eyes begged Brian to bear with Jump's mood.

It wasn't going to be easy, he thought. Well, at least the little one, Eddie, seemed to like him. He answered her with a nod.

CHAPTER
FIVE

Hildy's cooking was everything that Sam Pearson had promised. The meat melted in Brian's mouth and the biscuits were almost light enough to float off his plate. But the company at the supper table was harsh and grating. Jump sullenly ignored Brian. Laurie made use of him to tease Hunt. Hunt didn't take to that, or to Brian, at all. Hildy tried her best to make Brian feel welcome and at ease but her efforts were too obvious. Eddie was the only one happily at ease at the table. He was going on roundup as wrangler this season. The prospect had him thoroughly excited. He accepted Brian at the table as he had accepted other hired hands in years past. As the youngest of the Pearson children, he was used to taking orders from grownups, be they family, neighbors, or hired men.

Once the meal was done, Hildy sent Eddie to fetch water for the morning. Brian volunteered to go with him.

The snow was falling in a thin mist. Not a star was showing overhead. Brian carried a lantern, a homemade one with shaved horn panes to shield the candle inside from the wind. It glowed warmly but gave little light.

Distantly, coyotes raised their lonely howls. The night was growing downright cold.

Eddie's enthusiasm was still warm. As he and Brian made their way through the darkness, he confided joyfully, "I never been on roundup before. I never wrangled. But I been working horses plenty around the ranch. I'm a good rider. I figure maybe I'll take up bronc busting when my legs get longer."

"That's rough work. Hard on a man's insides."

"Do you ride broncs, Mister Brian?"

"I've rode the rough string a few places I've worked, but I'd sooner not bust up my guts doing it regular." Brian peered into the darkness ahead. "Ain't we about to that creek?"

"It's right over here." Eddie trotted ahead.

Brian saw the stream, a dark streak meandering through the pale crust of snow. Hunkering, Eddie dipped a bucket into it. Then the other. He rose with a bail in each hand, staggering some under the weight of the big wooden buckets.

"Here," Brian said, holding the lantern out to him. "You carry this. I'll fetch the water."

"I can handle it."

"Be easier for me."

Eddie shook his head. "I got it all right. It's my job. I can do it."

Brian didn't argue. The boy was proudly eager to do his share of the work. Hildy wouldn't have sent him for the water if it was too much for him. Carrying the lantern, Brian fell in at the boy's side.

"Who all goes on roundup together?" he asked.

"Mister Bailey and Teddy and Fletch and Buck. That's Mister Bailey's boys. Fletch is oldest. Teddy's almost as old. He's married, just got a new baby. Buck's about Jump's age. He rides nighthawk," Eddie said. "Then there's Mister Hunt and Pike Coster. Mister Coster is Mister Hunt's regular hired hand, works for him all year around. Mister Hunt hires on a man besides in the summer. Sometimes two men. He only hired one last year. Man name of Jones. Mister Jones got drunk and fell off his horse and spooked a gather and Mister Hunt fired him and didn't have extra help for all the rest of the summer. Mister Hunt says it's awful hard to get *good* help."

"It ain't hard for a *good* outfit," Brian commented. "Anybody else go along?"

"Let's see. There's the Baileys and Mister Hunt and his men and us. I reckon that's all."

"That's four Baileys and Hunt and Coster and a hired man, maybe two. Right?"

"Uh-huh. And us."

"Seven of them and you and me and Jump makes ten. Right?"

Eddie hesitated, studying on the sum, before he agreed, "Right!"

"Two wranglers and eight riders. Maybe nine," Brian said. It wasn't a very big outfit.

"Right," Eddie said as he climbed the steps to the cabin. He put down a bucket to open the door. Picking it up again, struggling with the weight, he shoved on in. Brian followed him.

Laurie was sitting on the sofa. Hunt perched on its arm, hovering over her. Both of them looked up as Eddie and Brian walked into the cabin. Hunt lifted a brow. "Bad back, Brian?"

"Huh?"

"I see you've let the boy do the *hard* work." Hunt nodded at the buckets Eddie was setting down near the fireplace. "Have you some physical disability?"

Laurie's mouth shaped a funny twisted little smile as she waited for Brian's answer.

"Or simple laziness?" Hunt added smugly.

Brian felt his face reddening. He was certain he had been right in letting Eddie do his own work himself. But now Hunt was making him look bad because of it. And Laurie's smile was making him feel like a damned fool.

Eddie interrupted before Brian could reply. Proudly, he said, "It ain't such hard work. Not for *me*."

Brian nodded.

"I suppose Brian had his hands full carrying the lantern," Hunt said.

Brian could feel the tension growing in his shoulders. His hands wanted to fist up and go for Hunt's face.

Looking into his eyes, Laurie stopped smiling. She changed the subject, speaking to Eddie. "Jump's upstairs waiting for you. You'd better get on up."

Eddie gave a disgusted grunt. He turned to Brian. "I got to go study. Ma makes Jump give me book lessons. She says if I don't do my learning here, she'll send me to stay in town and go to school there. I don't know

60

what I need with book lessons. I'm gonna be a bronc buster. You don't have to read books to ride broncs."

"It don't hurt none," Brian said, snuffing the lantern candle.

"But what *good* does it do?" Eddie protested.

"Well, a man who busts broncs, generally he gets paid by the head. He needs sums to tally up his wage."

"I can work sums."

"And if he gets himself busted up, it's right handy for him to be able to read. Kills time while he's healing."

"I ain't gonna get busted up."

"Every bronc rider does eventually."

Eddie looked to Hunt. "That so?"

"Probably," Hunt said. "The average bronc rider, the average cowhand, doesn't have sense enough to take care of himself."

Brian looked askance at Hunt. He saw Laurie watching him with a hint of that teasing little smile on her face again, as if she enjoyed seeing him insulted.

"You take your average no-account drifter," Hunt was saying to Eddie. "He hasn't sense enough to hold on to the money he makes and invest it in something worthwhile like land and cattle of his own. He isn't man enough to find himself a good woman and settle down. By the time he's my age, he's nothing but a broken-down, drunken bum, not good for anything."

"Not me!" Eddie answered. "I'm gonna bust broncs and make a lot of money and buy a whole herd of Durhams for Pa and Ma!"

"And get married?" Laurie said.

Eddie sighed. "A man doesn't *have* to get married if he don't want to. Does he, Mister Brian?"

Laurie eyed Brian curiously.

Brian gave the boy no reply.

Hunt said, "Some men aren't fit to be married. Only a woman with no wits about her at all would take a fancy to a no-good drifter."

The anger burning in Brian flared. He knew he had to cool it down or it might overwhelm him. Turning his back to Laurie and Hunt, he hung the lantern on the hook, then jerked open the door and stepped out into the chill privacy of the night.

The wind stung his face. Ducking his chin, he moved cautiously through the darkness. The hound came from under the steps and followed him as he made his way to the corrals. For a while he stood leaning on a rail smelling the scent of the horses and trying to think about the work ahead. But it was too cold for loafing. And his thoughts insisted on turning to Laurie Pearson. Disgusted, he stuffed his hands into his pockets and began to walk to keep warm.

Suddenly the cabin door opened. Halting, Brian turned and saw Laurie and Hunt silhouetted in the doorway. The hound trotted to meet them as they stepped outside. Laurie closed the door behind them. Hunt was carrying the homemade lantern in his hand.

"Why, Frank! I do believe you're jealous!" Laurie said as they headed across the yard toward the corral. They were unaware of Brian standing silent in the darkness not far beyond the lantern's feeble glow.

"Jealous of what?" Hunt grunted. "Some damned ragged-rumped saddle tramp who can't keep two bits in his poke? You know where he'll be when the work's done this fall? In a saloon with some waiter girl picking his pockets. *If* it takes him till fall to get there. You'll be lucky if he doesn't just up and disappear one morning when there's work to be done, and you never see him again. Or maybe you'd be lucky if he does. You'd be better off rid of him."

"What makes you think that?" she asked. "Why should Brian be worse than any other hired hand?"

Damned interested, Brian followed quietly along within earshot.

"They're none of them any good," Hunt told the girl. "They're all wild, irresponsible men who don't care about anything but drinking and gambling and wenching."

"*All* of them?" Laurie's tone was teasing. "Even Pike Coster?"

"Pike's different!" Hunt answered indignantly. "He was in the Army. He served under me. He isn't a drifter. He's a full-time working ranch hand. He has character and ambition."

"What makes you so sure Brian doesn't have character and ambition?"

"Just look at him! He's as filthy ragged as a worn-out scarecrow. He has nothing to his name but a saddle and a gun and a bonerack of a horse. His kind tramps from place to place doing a little work here and there in the summer, and begging keep in the winter. He's probably running from the law somewhere. Laurie, how can your mother even think of entrusting the roundup to a man like that?"

Brian felt an urge to butt in and explain himself. He was ragged and his horse was gaunted because they had just made one hell of a hard ride over Ade's Ridge. He only had one horse because he'd lost the other, along with most of his belongings, in an avalanche. He had never in his life begged a meal. He had paid in cash or work for every mouthful of food he had ever eaten. There wasn't a lawman in the land he wouldn't gladly give a "Good morning" and expect the same back from. Hunt was bad-mouthing him without any damned grounds at all.

But to speak out then and there would be to admit he had been eavesdropping. Sneaking around in the dark like a coyote stealing words that weren't meant for him. That was a shameful thing for a man to do.

Embarrassed at his own actions, he paused to consider the things that Hunt had said about him. He had to allow there might be a little truth in some of them. When the work was done in the fall, he did head straight for town, for a drink and a game and a warm bed. The waiter girls did pick his pockets one way or another. More than once he had hit town in early winter with his poke full and ended up dead broke by spring hiring with his saddle in hock. He'd had to borrow money from the girls to get it back so that he could work the summer.

With a scowl, he asked himself if any of the other things Hunt had said might be true.

Dammit, he always paid his debts. He always did the job he hired on to do. He had never gone back on his word or let down a friend who was depending on him. What more did the world want of a man?

Laurie and Hunt walked on to the corral. She held the lantern while he saddled up. He mounted, then leaned from his horse to speak softly to her.

She laughed.

Brian wondered what had been said. Likely it was some joke at his expense, he supposed. He felt an urge to move closer and hear whatever else might be said.

Hunt touched Laurie's cheek. He looked of a mind to kiss her. She looked of a mind to accept the kiss if it came.

Brian swallowed hard at the urge to interfere. It was none of his business, he told himself. Angry at his own thoughts, he wheeled sharply away.

The hound was lingering at Laurie's side. Brian's sudden move caught its attention. As it recognized his scent, it made a small noise of friendly greeting.

Lifting the lantern head-high, Laurie turned to peer into the darkness. "Hello? Is somebody there?"

"It's only me," Brian muttered, feeling the heat of embarrassment flush his face. He walked toward the girl, but halted at the edge of the lantern glow, barely visible to her.

"What are you doing here?" Hunt snapped at him. "Spying on us?"

The anger that burned in Brian was aimed partly at Hunt and partly at himself because Hunt was right. He had been spying. He had no intention of admitting it to

Hunt though. He said, "There were some Indians around here today. I thought somebody ought to walk Miss Laurie back to the cabin."

"Why, thank you, Brian," Laurie said with that funny little smile of hers.

Hunt grumbled, *"I'll* see Miss Pearson back to the cabin."

"No need," Brian said. "I'm here now. I'll do it."

"I'll do it," Hunt answered.

Laurie turned her teasing smile toward Hunt. "No, don't trouble yourself, Frank. Brian can see me back."

Hunt glared at Brian. Touching his hatbrim to Laurie, he lifted rein. As he gigged his horse into a trot, he called to her, "Just you remember what I said!"

Brian stepped to her side and asked her, "Remember what?"

She cocked a brow at him. "I'm afraid Frank hasn't taken much of a liking to you."

"Fair enough," Brian said, taking the lantern from her hand. He held it out, leading her toward the cabin.

As she fell in at his side, she told him, "Frank really is nice. You'll like him once you get to know him."

He didn't answer. After a moment, he said bluntly, "You plan to marry him?"

"I don't know. He wants me to."

"Do you want to?"

"I don't know." She looked askance at him. "Have you ever been in love, Brian?"

The question roused memories that almost brought a grin. He replied, "I never had any notion to get married about it."

She spoke into the darkness. "How is a person to know if she's in love or not? I mean, sometimes you think you are, and sometimes you think you aren't. How are you to be sure?"

"Seems to me if you ain't really sure, you ain't really in love."

"That's just about the same thing Ma says. She says when the time comes I won't have to ask."

"Likely she's right."

"I don't know. It's a puzzlement." She had reached the stoop. She put a foot on the bottom step and halted. The hound rubbed against her leg. She bent to pat its head. Looking down at the dog, she said to Brian, "Will you walk with me for a few minutes?"

"Ain't you cold?"

"I won't be if I keep walking. Come on. I don't want to go in just yet."

"Yes, ma'am."

With her hands stuffed into the pockets of her coat and her head ducked against the night wind, Laurie strode off across the yard. Pacing along at her side, Brian held the lantern out to light her way. The hound followed after them.

Thoughtfully, she said, "You know he's been married before?"

"I didn't know."

"Yes. When he was in the Army. She was a colonel's daughter. She was very pretty. He has a picture of her. Not a painting. One of those photograph things they make straight from a person's face. She was all done up in lace and frills when she sat for it. She had a very pale face."

"She's gone now?"

"Dead."

"How did she come to die?"

"A fever. Frank says she wasted away. But she was very pretty when the picture was made. Only she was older than I am. She'd be a lot older now. Maybe she wouldn't be so pretty now."

"I don't expect she was ever any prettier than you are," Brian said.

Laurie shook her head. There was a wistful sadness in her voice. "I'm not pretty. I'm all sunburned and my hands are callused like a man's and my hair won't hold a curl."

"What's wrong with that?"

"It's not *pretty!*"

"There's a lot more than one kind of pretty," he said. "A red heifer in a green field is real pretty. So's a tooled saddle with silver conchos. But they're right different things."

Laurie looked at him from the corner of an eye. The sadness went out of her voice, replaced by a hint of teasing. "Am I as pretty as a red heifer in a green field?"

"Ma'am," he said with mock solemnity, "you're as pretty as a red heifer wearing a silver saddle."

She laughed lightly. But then the wistful quality returned. "I'm not anywhere as pretty as Missus Hunt was. I don't have any fancy clothes with lace and frills, and if I did, I reckon I'd look downright silly in them. I don't know all those fine things a lady like her would

68

know. I've had some schooling and I've read some books and I know those people like that are different from me and my folks."

"You reckon any of those fine ladies could ride that zebra dun of yours, or rope a steer the way you can do?"

"I don't reckon any of them would even want to try."

"Then what good would they be around a ranch?"

She thought about it as they walked through the night. After a few minutes, she spoke. Her tone was soft and uncertain. "I don't know. I just don't know."

"There ain't no need to get all worried up now, is there?" he said. "You got a piece of time to make your mind up about Hunt. Your ma says you're going off to school back East come winter."

"Uh-huh. I think so."

"I thought you had it all planned."

"We did, but since Pa got hurt, I'm not sure. Maybe I ought to stay here with him."

"He'll be healed by then."

"But —" She hesitated. "The truth is, I'm not sure about the money. With the bull dead and Pa hurt and all, things ain't as good as they were. Maybe there won't be enough money for me to go to school."

"Your pa being laid up won't change the beef tally."

"No," she said slowly, doubtfully.

Brian could guess at her unspoken thoughts. Losing the bull meant next year's calf crop wouldn't be of the quality they had anticipated. Her father's injury meant hiring a man to work the summer. The hand's wage would have to come out of the year's earnings. How much those earnings came to would depend a lot on how good the hired hand was.

"Ma'am, I'm a top hand," he heard himself saying. "I know my trade. I never rode as a foreman before, but I know the work. I reckon I can get your calves branded and your beef to market."

"You won't up and leave us before the work's all done?"

"Is that what Hunt wanted you to keep in mind?"

"He said you'd get a hankering for a bottle or something and run out on us," she admitted.

"What do you think?"

"I don't know, Brian! There's so much I just don't know!"

He heard the pain and worry in her voice. It cut deep into him. Firmly, he said, "Well, you stop fretting about it. You got my word."

She touched his hand. Just for a moment her fingers clasped his, pressing hard as she accepted his promise.

Somewhere in the hills a coyote howled. The wild free voice told him that he had lost his own freedom. With a few short words, he had bound himself to a bigger job than he had ever wanted. The thought was cold and a little frightening. But the touch of Laurie's hand on his was very warm.

CHAPTER
SIX

The horses for the roundup had to be brought in from the range. Only a few using horses had been corralled at the ranch, hayed, and grained through the winter. The rest had been loosed when the work was done in the fall. They scattered in bunches, sometimes mixing with stock from the other ranches. They had to be gathered, sorted, and driven back to the corrals.

Packing bedrolls and supplies enough for several days, Brian and Jump set out at dawn to fetch them in. They rode with the sun at their backs, their shadows stretched out ahead of them. The snow hadn't lasted the night. By the time the sun was well clear of the horizon most of it was gone. The breeze was chill but not cold. It was a good day for work.

Brian's belly was comfortably full. The horse under him was fresh and lively. He would have felt fine but for one thing. At his side, Jump rode in sullen silence like a dull, dark cloud. Brian had a feeling it was going to be damned hard to work with, and look after, the boy.

He didn't like the idea of looking after Jump. He had no idea how to go about it. He couldn't see why a boy Jump's age couldn't take care of himself. But in a private moment before he left the ranch, Hildy had

71

drawn him aside and made a point of asking him to do it. Solemnly she had spoken of Sam's accident and the possible dangers on the range. She'd told Brian that she was depending on him to see to it that nothing bad happened to Jump.

He chafed under the memory of her words. She had put a heavy responsibility on him. He would almost sooner have gone after the horses alone than ride with such a burden.

They hadn't been traveling long when they cut horse sign. The trail angled ahead of them. As Brian reined to follow, Jump held back.

"Come on," Brian called to him.

"No. I'm going on ahead and have a look at the dead bull first."

"You're coming with me now."

Jump shook his head defiantly.

"Come on. We got work to do. We came out here to fetch in the horses."

"We'll get them in. Only first I'm going to see that bull," Jump insisted.

Brian rode back to his side. "You're coming with me now after this bunch."

"You go on. I'll catch up," Jump said.

"Sure!" Brian snapped, rankled. "You'll show up after I've got the work all done."

"I'll do my share! Only I mean to see that bull first!" Jump growled. He started to lift rein.

Brian grabbed the boy's horse by the bridle. "You're coming with me!"

"Are you afraid for me to look at the bull? Are you afraid I'll see something you don't want me to see? Is there something might tell me who shot our bull?"

The anger growing in Brian pulled his jaw taut as he answered, "There ain't nothing to see! It's just a dead carcass. You've seen dead carcasses before, ain't you?"

"Not this one!" Jump jerked at the reins, trying to pull the horse's head free of Brian's grip. The horse snorted and twisted in confused protest.

Brian's mount began to dance. His fingers slipped on the bridle. Hanging onto it, he was being pulled askew in his saddle. He grunted, "Boy, you're staying where I can keep an eye on you!"

"Like hell I am!" Jump lashed out with his rein ends.

The leather stung across Brian's face like the cut of a quirt. Wincing, he lost his grip on the bridle. Jump wheeled the horse away from him, slamming spurs into its flanks. It leaped into a gallop.

Upset, Brian's horse ducked its head and flung up its heels. Taken off-balance, Brian almost came unglued. By the time he had the horse in hand and his seat firm again, Jump was well away.

Hesitating, Brian rubbed at his stinging face. Dammit, the boy was old enough and experienced enough to ride off by himself. What the hell could happen? And it looked like the only way to hold him would be to hog-tie him.

Rising in the stirrups, he shouted after Jump, "You mind you catch up! Mind you don't get hurt or nothing!"

He knew Jump heard. He could see the boy tense. But Jump didn't look back or reply.

Disgusted with Jump for his behavior, with Hildy for saddling him with the responsibility for the boy, and with himself for failing to keep Jump in hand, Brian turned to follow the horse herd alone.

The sign was a couple of days old. The horses had been drifting slowly, grazing as they traveled. He followed their trail at the easy trot that covered ground without tiring a mount unnecessarily. Around noon, he found fresh droppings. A few minutes later, he spotted the bunch.

The horses were on a sunny slope where the grass was early and good. They were spread out, all facing uphill, grazing peacefully. He halted on a rise overlooking them. The breeze was coming from his right and a bit ahead of him. It carried his scent away from the horses. He figured if he rode to the left, staying behind the rise until he was down a ways, then cut across to a stand of trees that rose along the crest of the far slope, they wouldn't become aware of him. He could ride through the woods to the far side of the bunch and haze them back in the direction he had come. Maybe by then Jump would catch up and give him a hand with them.

He reached the woods without any trouble and was working his mount through the winter windfalls when he heard a calf bawling. It sounded like an orphan lost off somewhere away to his side. With a flick of the reins, he turned to hunt it.

He came suddenly to the edge of a ravine. The walls dropped sharply to a bottom a good couple of dozen feet below. The calf was in the ravine. So was a cow. The cow lay helplessly on its side, legs outthrust. From the rim of the ravine he couldn't tell whether it was hurt or had fallen with its hoofs higher than its body and just couldn't get itself up again.

He rode the rim, looking for a way down. Once he was sure he would be able to get himself and his mount up again, he gave the horse a nudge of his spurs. Scrambling and sliding on its haunches, the horse reached the bottom of the ravine.

The calf spooked at Brian's sudden arrival. It stopped its hollering and ran around to the far side of the cow.

The cow was aware of Brian but it barely lifted its head. Approaching it, he saw blood on its side and pink foam at its nostrils. A punctured lung, he thought. That was as good as dead. But he had to be sure before he put the animal out of its misery.

He had pigging strings in his pocket. Sorting one out of the bundle, he put it between his teeth. Lass rope in hand, he circled in toward the cow and calf.

As the rider neared it, the calf backed away. It kept close to the cow. Too close for Brian to heel it. With a twist of his wrist, he sent his loop rolling down the rope at its head. The loop dropped true. He snapped it closed around the calf's throat.

Gently, he backed his horse. The calf struggled at the end of the rope, but the steady tug brought it along. Once it was well clear of the cow, Brian halted. The horse held the rope taut as he stepped down from the saddle. The calf cowered fearfully as he walked up to it.

Standing at its side, he spoke soothingly to it. Suddenly, he reached across its back and flanked it down. Holding it on the ground with one hand and his legs, he took the pigging string from his teeth and got a wrap on a foreleg. Then he pulled in the hind legs and lashed them to the foreleg. Hog-tied, the calf lay helpless. Again, it was bawling. This time with frightened despair.

The sound of the cries stirred life in the cow. It struggled, trying to haul itself up. With a fierce effort it got its legs under it. Its rump rose. Swayed. And fell. Breath gurgling in its windpipe, it lay still.

Brian drew and cocked his revolver.

The cow made another try at rising as he approached it. It got its head off the ground. The foam at its nostrils was running red now. Its glazed eyes rolled wildly. It shook its head, showing him its horns, wanting to hook one into him. Blood driped from its muzzle.

"You got guts, old gal," Brian said. Certain there was no hope for the cow, he pointed his gun at its head. "Die proud."

The shot rang shockingly loud within the hollow of the ravine. The calf stopped bawling. It lay taut in silent fear.

The cow was dead. Hunkering beside it, Brian looked first at the earmarks and brand. Jinglebobs right and left and a box B on its flank. That was the brand Hildy had told him belonged to the Baileys.

He bent closer to examine the bloodstained body. Broken bone poked through torn flesh and hide. There was no trace of a bullet wound such as had killed the Pearsons' bull. No sign of anything unnatural. It seemed the cow had simply suffered an accident. Most likely it had fallen into the ravine. And the calf had followed its mother down.

Brian knew the cow should be skinned, the hide salvaged. But Box B wasn't the brand he rode for. Time was short. He had a lot of work to get done. The best he figured he could do for the neighbor who owned the cow was get the calf up out of the ravine. He decided the easiest way to do that would be to let it ride up on horseback.

Fishing another pigging string from his pocket, he retied the calf's leg, this time front to front and back to back. He lifted the calf in his arms and draped it over his saddle. He lashed it on, tied up the reins, and looped his lass rope over the horse's neck. Leading the horse, he started up the wall of the ravine afoot. The horse scrambled up after him.

On the rim again, he pulled the calf from the saddle. It was a sturdy little he-calf, old enough to have begun nibbling grass. If the wolves didn't pull it down, he figured it should be able to survive on its own. He sure as hell didn't have time to nursemaid it.

If it did survive, running loose without its mother, it could be picked up as a maverick and branded by the first man who dropped a loop on it. So it should be marked to show its rightful owner. He could do that much for Bailey.

There was no need to heat a cinch ring and run a brand on the calf. Earmarks would do until it was gathered in the roundup. He pulled out his knife and tested the edge. Kneeling at the calf's side, he caught up an ear.

Lead spanged past his head. It furrowed the ground just beyond him.

With a startled wince, he dropped the knife. As he slammed himself face down in the dirt, he glimpsed two men on horseback coming toward him. Hitting ground, he rolled to be well away from the spot where he had been, in case there was a second bullet.

The men didn't fire again. He understood then that they had meant to scare him, not kill him. Coming up onto his feet, he spread his hands to show them empty. He held them shoulder-high as he faced the two riders.

Both carried rifles. Both were pointing them at him.

"Hold on there!" he called, gazing at the round black eye of the nearest rifle. It stared back at him, looking hot and hungry.

The leading rider was the older of the two, a once-wiry man now past his prime, turning grizzled and gnarled. Eyes that were sun-faded but still sharp peered from a weather-hardened face. Strands of pale gray hair poked from under a well-worn Stetson. The mustache drooping over the mouth was streaked with white, stained with yellow at the edges from tobacco. The mouth was set in a thin, grim line.

The second rider was young and lean, with the shoulders of a bull-wrestler. His hat was cocked back on his head, showing a thatch of curly yellow hair. His mustache and brows were sun-bleached almost colorless. There was a pleasant, easygoing look to his eyes, as if he would be a good man to enjoy a few drinks with. He held his rifle casually, looking like he really didn't want to use it.

The older man snapped at Brian, "What the hell you think you're doing?"

Brian shrugged a shoulder at the hog-tied calf. "I'm ear-marking an orphan. Jinglebobs. For the Box B brand."

The rider squinted suspiciously at him. "Why for the Box B?"

"That's the brand its momma wore."

"You ride for the Box B?"

"No."

"I know damned well you don't!" the rifleman snapped, sounding as if Brian had claimed otherwise. "I own the Box B. I'm Ed Bailey. Who the hell are you?"

"Name's Brian. I'm riding for Sam Pearson's Forked P."

"You missed that loop, mister. You want to try again?"

"Huh?"

"Sam Pearson said he wasn't hiring any help this season. You're not riding for him."

"I am," Brian protested. "Sam got hurt and can't ride the roundup, so Missus Pearson hired me on."

The younger rider nodded as if he believed it. Brian glanced at him, wondering who he was. He didn't look kin to Bailey. Eddie had said Bailey's only riders were his sons.

Bailey spoke to Brian. "You tell me again what mark you meant to put on that calf."

"Jinglebobs right and left. Same as the cow was wearing."

"Where is the cow?"

"Down the ravine there. She's dead meat now. I'd have taken the hide for you, but there ain't time. I got to get the Pearsons' horses in for roundup."

"What did she die of?"

"Busted ribs."

Bailey turned to his companion. "Pike, would you mind going down, having a look for me?"

"Sure." The younger man reined his horse to the rim of the ravine and slummed it on down.

Brian looked at Bailey. "His name is Pike?"

Bailey nodded warily, as if he didn't like making any admissions of any kind to this stranger. He seemed to be of the common run of small ranchers, a cowhand who had finally set up a spread of his own. Likely he was a decent enough sort, but he was suspicious as hell of the stranger who had tied down one of his calves.

Brian asked, "Pike like the Pike Coster who works for Frank Hunt?"

"You know Frank Hunt?" Bailey grunted.

"I've met him. I thought Pike Coster was gone to fetch a doctor for Sam Pearson." There was anxiety in Brian's voice. Sam needed that doctor. Pike Coster had no business being out here when he should be on his way to fetch help.

Brian's question, and his tone, eased some of Bailey's wariness. "Pike come by my place and I sent my boy

Fletch on the rest of the way. With luck, the doc'll be to Sam's tomorrow or the next day."

Brian sighed with relief.

"You say you're working for Sam?" Bailey said.

"Missus Pearson hired me on yesterday."

"You never worked for Sam before?"

"No."

"How come her to hire *you?*"

"Happened I was handy."

Bailey gave the calf a glance. "Might be you're a bit too handy. What mark did you say you were putting on that doughgut?"

"Jinglebobs right and left for the Box B," Brian said once again.

Pike came scrambling his horse out of the ravine. He told Bailey, "It's one of your cows all right. And it's got busted ribs all right. Poked clear through the hide. It's got a bullet hole in its head, too."

Bailey scowled at Brian, his hand tensing on the rifle. "A bullet?"

"She wasn't dead when I found her," Brian explained. "I finished her."

"That's the way it looks," Pike agreed. "Lots of blood around the busted ribs, mostly dried up and caked. Not much blood around the bullet hole, but it's fresh. I think he's telling the truth."

"But the calf?" Bailey said. "How the hell can I tell if he's telling the truth about how he meant to mark the calf?"

"Want to watch me do it?" Brian suggested.

"Hell, man, I don't doubt you'll jinglebob it now. But how do I know you meant to do that all along?"

"Because you got my word on it."

"How do I know your word's good?"

Anger surged in Brian. Tautly, he said, "You ask anybody I ever rode for. Ask the men I've rode with. Ask the girls up to Tallow Dip. They know me."

Pike grinned.

"Tallow Dip's a far piece to ride right now," Bailey grunted skeptically.

"Look here," Brian said, "I'm getting fed up with this. I got work to do. The Pearson's are shorthanded. I ain't but one man. I've got to get the horses in and ready for roundup. I've wasted a lot of time saving that calf for you, and a lot more standing here auguring you. I ain't got no more to waste. You can mark your own damned calf!"

Turning, he grabbed for the reins of his horse.

"Hold on!" Bailey snapped at him.

Brian halted and looked back over his shoulder at Bailey's rifle. It was raised and ready.

"Bailey," Pike said quietly, "you got a burr under your tail or something? This here feller is just trying to do a job of work, same as the rest of us, and you're giving him hell over it."

Bailey frowned. He eased back a bit as he said, "The boys and me been hunting horses too. We've been seeing cattle, but not nearly as many as we ought to be seeing. It's like somebody's been thinning the herd for us. I don't like it one damned bit!"

"Maybe you just ain't looked in the right places yet," Pike suggested. "Maybe the beef's drifted in a different direction this past winter. Likely they'll turn up all right come roundup."

"Maybe." Bailey sounded doubtful.

Pike turned to Brian. "Mister, if you're after the Pearson horses, I'll give you a hand. I'll help you run them back to the ranch. If it's for the Pearson's, Frank won't mind."

The mention of Frank Hunt stiffened Brian's spine. He appreciated Pike's offer. But Pike was Hunt's man. Brian wanted no help from Hunt or his hired hands. He gave a shake of his head. "I can handle them."

Suspicion flared again in Bailey's eyes. "You don't want Pike riding along with you?"

"I wouldn't want to put him out," Brian grumbled. "I reckon he's got work of his own."

Pike nodded slightly.

Testing Brian with the question, Bailey asked, "You want to throw in with me and my boys? We can gather our horses together, then separate them out and run them to where they belong."

That was a good idea, Brian thought. It would be a lot easier than working alone, or with Jump sulking at his side. "I'd be obliged."

Bailey's suspicion turned to puzzlement. If Brian was a long-roper, he shouldn't want to join anybody's camp. So maybe Brian wasn't a long-roper. Maybe Brian was just what he claimed to be. Bailey gave a shake of his head. Then he shrugged. "Well, go ahead and earmark that calf and come on. We all got work to do."

Hunkering, Brian recovered his knife. He caught one of the calf's ears and slit it so that the lower part would hang as a jinglebob. When he had cut the other ear, he pulled loose his pigging strings. The calf staggered to its feet with a bellow for its mother.

Brian collected his horse and stepped aboard. He reined the horse in between the calf and the rim of the ravine. The calf backed away from him. He moved toward it, keeping it going. It would have to be driven some distance or it would try going back to the dead cow.

"Bailey," Pike said. "I ought to get back to the ranch. We got to start bringing our own horses in. But I'll take that hide for you first. I'll fetch it to you next time I'm by your way."

"Much obliged," Bailey replied. He kicked his horse into a lope. Falling in next to Brian, he said, "Nice feller, Pike Coster."

"Is he?" Brian grunted.

"Him and Hunt both. Good neighbors."

Brian made no reply to that.

After a moment, Bailey asked, "How bad is Sam hurt?"

Brian thought if he was going to hunt horses and ride roundup with Bailey, he ought to get friendly with the man. He told Bailey about the accident, then volunteered some information about himself and how he had come to the Pearson place.

As they talked, Bailey's distrust of Brian seemed to ebb. After a while, Brian asked, "You get much trouble from long-ropers around here?"

Bailey shrugged. "It ain't been usual. I don't know if we're really having it now or not. But me and my boys been hunting horses all morning and most of the cattle we been seeing is she-stuff and calves. It just don't seem like we're seeing the beef steers the way we should. Not at all. Not the way we should."

"You think you're missing stock?"

"It's awful early to say yet, but I got a feeling of it. Dammit, we had a good winter. Not enough bad weather for a die-off. Last time I rode out, I seen plenty of beef on the hoof. Now it's like somebody was riding just a step ahead of us, driving off our beef. Hell, I don't know!" Bailey shook his head in puzzlement. Then he looked sharply at Brian. He patted the gun on his hip as he added, "But I'll find out! If I tally short come roundup, I'll sure as hell find out why!"

CHAPTER
SEVEN

Brian and Bailey were just moving in on the band of horses that Brian had spotted, when Jump caught up. Sullenly, Jump admitted he hadn't found any more sign around the carcass of the bull than Brian had described.

"I told you that you wouldn't," Brian said. "Now, you get on and help us with these horses. And be careful you don't get hurt."

Glowering, Jump took his place.

As they moved the horses toward Bailey's camp, Jump rode with reckless abandon. When Brian called him down for it, he just got worse about it. By the time they got the horses to the camp, Brian felt drawn taut with worrying about the boy. Angry and sullen himself, he was close to ordering Jump to quit the work and go back home.

Drawing him aside, Bailey told him, "You're being too rough on that boy, Brian. He knows the work. Let him alone and he'll do it all right."

"He's going to break his fool neck," Brian answered.

"He's riding rough because you're giving him a hard time. You're treating him like he doesn't know anything. Let him alone. He'll settle all right."

"I got to look out for him. I promised his ma I would."

"You don't have to wet-nurse him."

"I promised his ma," Brian repeated.

With a shrug, Bailey let it go.

The next morning, Bailey suggested Jump ride with him and Brian take one of his sons as partner. Brian liked the idea. But he had promised Hildy he would look after Jump. He kept the boy with him. And they kept fighting.

Except for the continual battle with Jump, the horse hunt went well. Bailey had two sons with him. Buck was close to Jump's age, shy with people but good with horses. Teddy was a year or two older than Brian. He had just become a father for the first time and was filled with the joy of it. He was so happy that it was hard for a man to stay sulky around him. The oldest boy, Fletch, joined them once he had seen the doctor to the Pearson place. He was a good hand, serious about the work and easygoing about everything else. Like his father, he felt there was beef missing off the range. It worried him, but not as much as it worried his father.

Once the horses were all bunched, they were separated by brand. The Rocking H stock that had been picked up was choused off toward Hunt's range, where his outfit would be looking for them. Brian and Jump cut out the Pearson horses, exchanged goodbyes with the Baileys, and headed back to the ranch.

As he herded them along, Brian observed the horses carefully. The ones unfit for work, the sore-footed or sickly or injured, would have to be doctored and then turned to range again. The rest would have to be shod. The feisty ones would have to be saddled a time or two to settle them for working the roundup.

As they neared the ranch, Laurie and Eddie rode out to meet them. Laurie brought news of Sam. The doctor had been and gone. He had done what he could and left instructions to keep Sam's wound clean, keep Sam warm and comfortable, and pray. He hadn't made any promises. Sam's recovery was in the hands of God.

Hildy spread a good table to welcome Brian and Jump back. She put on a bright, cheerful face to go with it. But Brian could see the weariness and worry in her eyes. After supper, she put Laurie to cleaning up, and went to sit with her husband.

Eddie and Jump disappeared into the loft.

Lingering at the table, Brian offered to help Laurie with her chores.

She was collecting the wreckage of the supper. Smiling in that teasing way of hers, she told him, "No, thank you, Brian. I wouldn't trust you to carry a china plate."

"Ma'am?" He looked askance at her, wondering if he was being insulted.

Her smile was warm and pleasant. "You look too tired to hang onto one."

He grinned back at her then. "I reckon I am. You've got a lively bunch of horses there."

"Did they give you a lot of trouble?"

"Nothing special, but they kept us busy. All the time we were trying to get them back to the ranch, they kept wanting to go wandering." He paused, then added, "I can't say I blame them."

Her smile weakened as she glanced at him. He realized she was remembering Hunt's warning that he would take off just when they needed him most. Defensively, he said, "I reckon them horses and me all got us a job to do before we go wandering off again."

With her back to him, Laurie asked, "Do you *have* to go wandering off again?"

"Ma'am?"

"Haven't you ever thought of staying put? Settling down in one place and staying there with a roof over your head in the winter and steady work in the summer?"

"No, ma'am. I reckon that ain't my way."

"Why not?"

"It just ain't."

"The horses settle down." She had dumped the dishes into a tub of soapy water. She scrubbed at them, keeping her back to Brian as she talked. "They stay pretty much on the same range every winter. They always come back to the same corrals and the same work in the summer."

He answered, "I ain't a horse."

"No!" She sounded surprisingly angry. "No, you're a mule!"

"Ma'am?"

"Nothing! Never mind!"

He slumped in his chair, frowning at her back as she worked.

Suddenly she said, "Frank Hunt was by today."

"Ain't he got any work of his own to do at his own place?" he grunted, rankled to have Hunt's name brought up.

She nodded. She didn't look at him as she said, "Frank cares more about me than he does his old work. He asked me again to marry him."

"What did you say?"

"What business is that of yours?"

He didn't answer. He had to allow to himself that it wasn't any of his business. Not unless he meant to throw a rope at her himself. And he sure didn't intend to go tying himself down to a woman. Not permanently.

She said nothing more, but hurriedly finished the dishes. She made a point of not looking at Brian as she turned to hang up her apron, then go into Sam's room. She avoided looking at him when she came out again and went up to her own room in the loft.

He sat gazing at the stairs she had climbed. Thoughts of her and Frank Hunt chased themselves through his mind. He seemed unable to rid himself of them.

After a while, he unrolled his soogans under the stairs. Snuffing the candle, he settled in. He should have slept instantly. His body was exhausted, aching for rest. But he lay with his eyes open to the darkness and thoughts of Laurie and Hunt persisting in his mind.

Eventually the thoughts became dreams. When he woke, he couldn't remember just what he had dreamed, only that he hadn't liked it at all.

By the time the sun poked up over the eastern ridge, breakfast was finished. Brian, Jump, and Eddie headed for the corrals to separate out the horses that needed doctoring. Along about midmorning, Laurie joined them.

Laurie didn't have to take part in the ranch work. Hildy made that clear to Brian. Laurie was not a cowhand. She had chores of her own at the house, and she would be needed to take on some of the work of nursing Sam. If she helped with the horses, it was of her own free will.

Brian felt a deep pleasure when she showed up dressed for work and offered to give a hand. It was fun watching her roping a horse from the herd. She moved with a quick grace, almost as if she were dancing. And she controlled her rope skillfully, setting it where she wanted it.

The work went well until midafternoon. Then Frank Hunt showed up. At his arrival, Laurie quit and went off with him. That roused a dark anger in Brian. He felt Hunt had no right interfering with the work. But Laurie wasn't a ranch hand. Brian couldn't call her down for walking off. He was helpless to stop her from lollygagging with Hunt.

Once the unfit horses had been tended and turned back onto the grass, strings had to be picked for the riders and readied for the roundup. Brian needed to know which horses were green and which experienced. There was no asking Jump. He was still as sulky as ever. But Eddie was eager to be helpful.

They had run the horses all together into one big corral. Brian and Eddie sat on the top rail, looking them over. Eddie pointed out each of them, giving Brian its history. Jump perched a short ways from them, listening but never offering a word or a sign that he overheard.

According to Eddie, some of the horses were completely green, never saddled before. Brian hoped he could make up strings without using any of them. He didn't have the time or inclination to start breaking in raw broncs before the roundup.

Most of the Pearson horses were half-made, ready to be worked, but ignorant of the work to be done. Such horses learned by doing. It was a rider's job to use them, educating them as he went along.

Some, but not enough, were well-made and experienced at the work.

Brian figured he would give Eddie the best-made of the horses and take half-made mounts into his own string. He wondered just what horses he dared give Jump. While they were bringing in the horses, Jump had ridden good using mounts. Brian had no idea how well Jump could handle a green horse. And he had promised Hildy that he would look out for the boy.

He was pondering the problem when Laurie came up. She was dressed for work. Hoisting herself onto the rail next to him, she smiled at him. "What's happening?"

"We're drawing our strings for the roundup!" Eddie grinned.

Brian asked her, "How good is Jump with rough stock?"

At the sound of his name, Jump tensed. He scowled as he looked at his sister from the corner of his eye.

"How do you mean?" she said to Brian.

"How good is he at riding green horses?"

Her mouth twisted with a hint of teasing. "He's *almost* as good as I am."

"I can ride any bronc you can, and half more besides!" Jump snapped at her.

"As long as it's got a hoof tied up," she answered.

Jump exploded. Anger flared in his face. Grabbing the rope from his saddle, he dropped into the corral.

"Hey!" Brian hollered, going after him.

The horses were crowded into the corral. They had been shuffling restlessly, not liking the tight pen after a winter of running free. As Jump hit the ground among them, the nearest shied away from him. They rammed rumps against the others, setting the whole bunch into spooky milling. A young bay, green and nervous, reared. That startled the horses around it into fear. Instantly, the fear spread. Suddenly all of the horses were thrashing, twisting, hunting some escape from the corral. All around Jump, horses were rearing, pawing the air.

Heedless, Jump began to build himself a loop.

Brian ducked between dancing legs and under horses' bellies, heading for the boy.

Jump discovered his danger. One horse was wheeling to fling its hind hoofs at him. He leaped back. The hoofs shot out, barely missing him. The horse behind him was startled by his sudden move. It went up, flailing its forehoofs at his back.

"Jump! Look out!" Laurie screeched.

He heard her. Turning, he saw the hoofs coming at him. As he threw himself to the side, the hoofs flashed past him.

The scream might have saved Jump's hide, but it panicked the horses. The one that had almost struck Jump reared to strike again. Others pushed and shoved frantically. One lunged teeth at another. The other backed. It jammed against Jump. His back was to its barrel. He had no room to run as the rearing horse started down, its hoofs aimed for his face.

Squirming among the horses, Brian reached the rearing animal. He flung himself past it, throwing himself at Jump's knees. As he hit the boy's legs, they buckled. As the rearing horse came down, Jump was flat on the ground. Brian was pulling him to the side, rolling with him. The hoofs slammed into the earth where Jump's chest had been an instant before.

Then the horse was rearing again, meaning to strike again, as if it were trying to trample a rattler. But now Jump was clear. Brian was shoving him under the bottom corral rail. And rolling out after him.

A hoof skinned along Brian's thigh. He felt it scrape as he twisted himself under the rail. Then he, too, was in the clear.

For a moment, both Brian and Jump lay breathless on the ground just outside the corral. Eddie and Laurie rushed to them. As Laurie reached his side, Brian was scrambling up. Laurie stopped. Brian was lunging at Jump. Snatching the front of Jump's jacket, Brian hauled the boy to his feet.

Jump still didn't have his breath. He was gasping as Brian glared at him.

For an instant, Laurie stood bewildered. Then she realized what was about to happen.

"No!" she screamed as Brian slammed a hard-knuckled fist at Jump's jaw.

As he struck, Brian let go Jump's jacket. The blow sent Jump stumbling backward. Tripping, the boy sprawled on the ground again.

Brian bent as if to grab him up and hit him again.

Laurie gripped Brian's arm. Her eyes blazed as she demanded, "What are you doing!"

Brian's gaze was steady on Jump. Jump was catching his breath and getting himself onto his feet. His hands fisted. Under dark smears of dirt, his face was drained pale, intense with anger and all of the resentment of Brian that had been building inside him. He lunged for Brian, both fists flying.

Brian pushed Laurie away and met Jump's attack.

It was no match. Brian had the advantage of reach, of weight, and of experience. He let Jump land a couple of blows. Good hard blows that hurt but that failed to throw him off balance. Then he swung his fist again, this time into Jump's breadbasket.

Jump went down. He stayed down, lying on his back, sucking jerky, pained little breaths.

"You're crazy!" Laurie shouted at Brian, trying to stop him by clinging to his arm. On the other side, Eddie was doing his best to hold Brian's other arm. Brian shook them both off. Laurie turned to Jump then. He was still down. She dropped to her knees at his side. "Are you hurt?"

"He ain't hurt," Brian grunted.

"You hit him!" Eddie hollered. He balled a fist and swung it at Brian's gut.

Brian caught the first, closing his hand over it. He pressured it enough to bring Eddie to a halt. "I'll hit you, too, if you ever try a damnfool stunt like your brother just did. He could have got killed."

Laurie glowered at Brian. "*You* could have killed him!"

Brian shook his head.

Jump struggled himself into a sitting position. With his arms pressed to his belly and his face mottled, he worked up enough voice to say, "I'll get you, Brian!"

"All right," Brian said coldly. "But you'd better wait until your pa's on his feet again or else you've got another hired hand to ride for you."

"No!" Laurie shouted. "We don't want you here any more, Brian! You're no good, like Frank said! We don't need you! Jump and I can ride the roundup!"

"Me, too!" Eddie put in.

"You get out," Laurie went on. "Get off our land! Don't ever show up around here again!"

Letting go Eddie's fist, Brian turned away. As he did it, he felt a dull pain in his left thigh. The soreness of a new bruise. He remembered the horse's hoof scraping down against his leg. Now the leg didn't want him walking on it. With a silent curse, he limped toward the cabin.

Hildy had heard the commotion. She had been late getting to the door for a look. She was just opening the door as Brian headed for it.

"What is it?" she said. "What's the matter?"

He gave a jerky nod toward Jump. "Your boy there just tried to get himself killed. I'm collecting my gear and pulling my stake."

"What? No! Why?"

Halting short of the stoop where she stood, he spoke across the distance to her. He called loudly enough for Laurie and the boys to hear him. "I can't ride with anybody I can't trust. Somebody who'd do a damnfool thing like he did, maybe get himself killed, maybe get me killed too. I don't mean to leave here in any more pieces than I came in."

He caught a breath, then added more quietly, "Ma'am, I can't work a ranch and ready up a bunch of half-green horses and nursemaid wet-eared young'uns all at once."

"Nursemaid?" Hildy frowned in question at him.

"You give me a crew of little boys I got to look after like I was to wipe their noses and button their britches for them, and I can't do it."

"I never — what on earth — ?"

"You said for me to look out for them. I can't do it all. They got to help. They got to try looking out for themselves," he grumbled.

Hildy lifted her eyes from his face to her children. She called, "Laurie, you come here! Jump! Eddie! All of you, come here! Now!"

Slowly, reluctantly, they obeyed. Jump walked with a pained stiffness, but he refused the support his sister offered him. Laurie stayed at his side, her hands hovering, ready to help him. Eddie walked along at his other side, offering his own small help.

When they were all lined up in front of her, Hildy scowled down from the stoop at them and said sharply, "Brian wants to quit."

"I fired him," Laurie answered defiantly, certain she was in the right.

"Why?"

Eddie spoke up. "He started in to hitting Jump!"

"What did you do?" Hildy demanded of Jump.

"I was just going to rope me out a horse and ride it, only *he* grabbed me and started beating on me!" Jump hooked an accusing thumb at Brian.

"Is that so, Brian?" Hildy asked.

Brian turned to Eddie. "What do *you* say?"

Eddie glanced from Brian to Jump and back again.

"Well?" Hildy insisted.

Sighing, Eddie said slowly, "Jump got down into the corral and the horses all went loco. I thought they were going to stomp him. Only Mister Brian piled in and fetched him out —"

"And attacked him!" Laurie interrupted. "Before poor Jump could hardly get his feet under him this — this — he —" She gave a jerk of her head toward Brian. "He attacked him! He hit him in the face!"

"With a fist?" Hildy asked.

Laurie nodded. Jump echoed the nod and rubbed his jaw.

Hildy turned to Jump. "What did you do then?"

"I hit him back!" Jump sounded very proud of himself.

"And then he hit Jump again!" Laurie put in. "He hit him right in the middle and knocked the breath out of him!"

Hildy lifted a brow. "You mean Brian fistfought him like he was a grown man?"

Laurie nodded vigorously, as if her point had been proven and her anger justified.

"Brian," Hildy said sternly, "that's where you did it wrong. You should have taken him over your knee and tanned his backside."

"*Ma!*" Jump screeched in protest.

Hildy answered him, "Jump, you may have size enough to ride the roundup, but maybe you ain't got sense enough. Maybe I'd better keep you here to fetch me firewood and send Eddie in your place."

Eddie puffed up, hopeful that she really would. He grabbed Brian's hand, pleading, "I'd behave, Mister Brian! I'd work hard and do real good! I promise!"

"Hush up," Hildy told him. Her eyes went to Brian, begging him to understand. She kept her voice soft, almost expressionless, letting her eyes say most of it. "Brian, I'd be obliged if you'd give us another chance. I never meant for you to nursemaid the boys, only just to guide them along where they're green and keep them from biting off too big a cud for their size. But if they act like they need nursemaiding, come roundup time I'll leave them here and I'll ride herd with you myself. I can't rope but if you'll heel them, I can flank them."

She looked as if she could, too. Suddenly Brian wasn't angry any more. He felt like grinning at her. Grinning with her.

And, hell, he couldn't just up and walk out on her after he had given her his word. Keeping his face straight and his tone solemn, he said, "Ma'am, I reckon you got a deal."

CHAPTER
EIGHT

The heavy leather chaps Brian had been wearing when he went into the corral after Jump had protected his leg from the blow of the horse's hoof. No skin was gone, no serious damage done. By morning he had a bruise on his thigh as big as his hand. His leg was sore, aching when he walked, but it wasn't bad enough to make him limp noticeably or to interfere with his work. He didn't mention it to anyone.

Jump showed up for breakfast carrying himself as if he had a bellyache. There was a purpling patch of bruise on his jaw that evidently hurt him when he chewed. He ate slowly, glancing at Brian now and then through sullen, slitted eyes.

This morning Laurie matched Jump's moody silence. The looks she gave Brian were every bit as dark and angry as Jump's. Something inside Brian winced each time she turned those accusing eyes on him.

Even Eddie felt the antagonism around him. He ate quietly, showing none of his usual exuberance for the day ahead.

But there was no time to waste in sulking. There was work to be done.

Once the horses had been culled, they had to be shod. Brian sent the boys to loop out individual horses, settle them a bit, and bring them to him at the anvil.

The first horse they brought him was a kicker. He had a fight getting a hoof tied up. Even balanced on three legs, the horse struggled as he cleaned each hoof and rasped it level. Pearson kept cold shoes as well as bar stock. The store-bought horseshoes were already shaped and punched for the nails. The man doing the shoeing only had to choose the right size and hammer the iron enough to shape it to the particular hoof.

The shoes seldom fit without reshaping. No man worth salt would ever file a hoof to fit a shoe. A misfit shoe or a badly driven nail would ruin a horse for the work, maybe ruin it forever.

It was a tiresome business, fighting the horses that were shy or ornery, preparing the hoofs, fitting the shoes, and nailing and clinching them. By the time Brian had one horse finished, the boys were waiting with the next. He began to feel like it was an endless parade of horses, each with its own problems and peculiarities. Shoe after shoe after shoe after shoe.

Despite the coolness of the day, by midafternoon he was dripping sweat. To break the monotony as well as to quench his thirst, he left the anvil to get himself a drink of water from the bucket by the cabin stoop. While he was drinking from the dipper, Hildy came to the door.

"Laurie's done her house chores," she told him. "You want her to come help with the horses?"

102

He looked askance at her, thinking of the dark scowls Laurie had given him at breakfast and again at nooning. "She willing?"

"Of course."

He doubted that. But there was work to be done, and plenty of it. He said, "If you can spare her, I'd be obliged. I got a job she can do."

After a few minutes, Laurie came to the door. She hadn't changed into her range clothes. She still wore the cotton dress and apron she had put on that morning for her household chores. Her face was stiff and her eyes were cold as she said to Brian, "You want me?"

"There's work to be done, if you're willing." He paused, hoping she would show some sign of being willing. She didn't. He went on, "The saddles all got to be gone over. Anything wearing out has to be patched up before we start riding these horses. You reckon you can do it?"

She nodded.

He pointed to the shed that served as a storeroom. "Mine's yonder. I know the rigging is worn. The leathers that hold the rigging rings need work. You got rivets?"

She shook her head.

"Then I reckon you'll have to punch them and lace on reinforcements. You know what I mean?"

Tight-lipped, she nodded. She seemed determined not to give him one word more than she had to.

"A man's life can depend on his saddle," he said.

She nodded again.

"Can you cut thongs?"

Another grim nod.

"You sure you understand what's got to be done?"

Still another stiff, silent nod that begrudged him the sound of her voice.

It was downright bothersome. She was making him feel uncomfortable as hell, almost as if he really had been wrong in hitting Jump. He heard himself say, "You know why I had to hit him, don't you?"

She wasn't willing to talk about it. Stiffly, she said, "I'll get to work."

Snatching her coat from the peg by the door, she hurried down the steps and on past Brian. She pulled the coat on as she trotted across the yard to the shed.

He felt a strong urge to follow her and try explaining to her about hitting Jump. He wanted her to understand how the boy had endangered himself, and the horses as well. He wanted her to know he had hit Jump to impress the boy with the seriousness of such a damnfool stunt. But he realized she had no intention of listening, no matter what he said.

He let her go on to the shed alone. Helping himself to another dipper of water, he splashed some into his face. Then he headed back to the anvil. The boys were waiting for him with another horse.

The afternoon was dragging slowly on when Frank Hunt came loping into the yard. He was riding a tall blood bay, looking as slick as if he were going to a meeting. He had on a black wool shortcoat and California striped pants. There was a soft tie at his throat and a silver band on his Stetson. He waved at the boys and went on to the cabin.

Dammit, Brian thought, didn't that bastard ever stay home and do his own work?

Hunt didn't visit with Hildy and Sam long. In a matter of minutes, he left the cabin and headed for the shed where Laurie was working on the saddles.

Brian kept hammering at the shoe he had on the anvil, but from the corner of an eye, he watched Hunt disappear into the shed. When he tried the shoe, he had hammered it too much. He had to work it back again.

After a while Hunt and Laurie left the shed together. The two of them strolled toward the corrals, chatting and laughing. Brian gave them a glance and pointedly went on with his work. They stopped short of him without speaking to him. He tried not to pay them any mind. But it riled him to have them standing watching him that way.

He finished with the horse he had at hand, and took the next one the boys brought. The boys collected the shod horse and started away with it.

"Hold on, boys," Hunt said, stepping out to intercept them.

"Sir?" Jump asked as he halted.

"Let's see what kind of work your new hired man does." Hunt bent and ran a hand down the horse's nigh foreleg. This was a made horse that had let itself be shod without a fuss. It stood as Hunt lifted the leg and examined the shoe critically.

Brian stopped work to watch.

Hunt lifted each of the horse's legs and looked at each shoe. He poked his finger at the frog of each hoof and ran his fingertip over each of the clinched nails. He studied the shoes as if he were desperate to find something wrong with them. Disappointed, he let down the last hoof without comment. As he straightened, he gave Brian a nod. It was the gesture of an overseer giving an untrustworthy underling permission to go on with a job.

Hunt's stance, his expression, his whole attitude, seemed purposely calculated to gall Brian. And he was succeeding. Brian felt anger knotting in his gut. His grip on the hammer tightened as his hand tried to fist itself.

Laurie's watching eyes were bright and vengeful. It was easy to see that she wanted Brian strung down a peg or two. She hoped Hunt would do it. Likely she had put Hunt up to it. Hunt seemed happy to go along.

Brian didn't mind a fight, but he didn't like the idea of being goaded into one like a buck flagged into a trap.

As if he thought Brian hadn't understood him, Hunt said, "The shoes are satisfactory. You may continue with your work."

Brian felt the heat in his face and knew his anger was showing. He saw Laurie's mouth shape a small smirk. But, dammit, he wasn't going to fight just to please her.

Tautly, he looked Hunt down, from the silver band on his Stetson to the polished toes of his Kansas City boots. He spoke slowly, his voice a soft, controlled drawl. "You ain't from Texas."

He said it as if that simple fact put Hunt beneath his consideration.

"Thank God, no!" Hunt snapped back scornfully.

Laurie was Texas-born herself, reared to the fierce pride of the Texan. She scowled at Hunt. "What's wrong with being from Texas?"

Hooking a thumb at Brian, Hunt started to speak. Then he realized Laurie was a Texan. Flustered, he stammered, "Why — uh — of course, there's nothing wrong with being from Texas."

"But you just said — !" She bit her words short as she realized Brian was beating her at her own game. She had meant to use Hunt against him. Now he was turning her against Hunt. For a moment she glared at him.

Then, stiffly, she said, "Come on, Frank."

Hunt hesitated, not yet ready to give up on Brian.

"Come on!" Laurie repeated impatiently. Her face was flushed and the hand she held out to Hunt was rigid. She made a sharp gesture with it.

Shrugging slightly to himself, Hunt turned his back on Brian. He took Laurie's hand in his. Holding it, he walked off with her.

Laurie glanced back over her shoulder.

Casually, Brian picked up a rasp and busied himself with the horse at hand. This was another gentle one, willing to be shod. Catching up a hoof, he tucked it between his legs and began to clean the frog. He looked as if his whole attention was on the job. But he was grinning slightly to himself.

CHAPTER
NINE

Once the horses were all shod, the winter kinks had to be ridden out of them. The day of the first saddling dawned damp and dreary. It had rained heavily during the night. The ground was a slop of mud. The sky was clearing, but a cutting chill edged the wind. Feeling it, the horses in the corral were restless and full of ginger.

Brian planned to ride first himself, then let Jump and Eddie each saddle a mount from his own string. The boys were ready to ride catch for him as he entered the corral, rope in hand. The horses eyed him warily as if they knew just what he had in mind. Backing and milling, they tried to hide behind each other.

His bruised leg was still stiff. He figured on starting with an easy horse, riding the stiffness out, before he forked any of the half-green broncs. The one he decided to begin with was a well-made bay gelding called Hug.

He never looked directly at Hug as he made his loop. He kept turned slightly away, facing a rawboned sorrel as if it were the horse he meant to take. The sorrel danced nervously under his gaze.

Suddenly he flicked his loop at Hug. At that moment, he saw Laurie from the corner of his eye.

Frank Hunt was with her. They were strolling toward the corral hand in hand.

Hug was wise in the ways of ropers. Seeing the loop coming, the horse wheeled on its haunches and spun away. The dampness didn't do a grass rope a bit of good. The loop ran slow. It fell short. Hug was out from under it. The horse's heels shot up in a buck of celebration as it ran from Brian.

A man missed a catch sometimes. Even the best roper on the range missed catches. But with Hunt and Laurie and the boys all watching him, Brian felt a surge of embarrassment. It was one hell of a rotten time to miss.

"You want a hand there?" Hunt called in mockery. "I'll be glad to catch him for you."

Angry as well as embarrassed, Brian ignored the remark. He built a new loop. As he turned toward Hug, he suddenly changed his mind about the horse. He figured Hunt had come to see him put on a show. Hunt probably hoped to see him eat dirt. All right, he'd put on a show, but not the one Hunt was hoping for. He'd show Hunt some damned fine riding.

He sent his loop flying for a dark brown four-year-old gelding called Snapper, a horse he knew was only half-broke.

Snapper was running. Brian's loop was suddenly in front of the horse's head. Before Snapper could realize what was happening, its head was through the loop and the loop was closing.

Twisting, Brian braced with his heels in the mud and his hips against the rope. The loop clamped tight on Snapper's throat.

Brian slid some in the mud as the rope went taut with Snapper's weight at the end of it. His heels dug in. Held. The horse's head swung around. Pivoting on the forehand, Snapper skidded in the mud. Scrambling, the horse managed to keep up. It caught balance and stood facing Brian along the length of the rope. Hand over hand, Brian took up rope as he approached the horse.

Jump was ready with a second loop. It would have been easy for him to drop it on the horse. Held from two directions, Snapper wouldn't have been able to put up much fight. But Brian gestured Jump's rope away. He meant to take Snapper without help.

As he neared the horse's head, Snapper went up into a rear. Ducking the flailing forehoofs, Brian got the bight of his rope over Snapper's poll. Tugging, he brought the horse down. As Snapper's hoofs hit ground, Brian gave the rope a twist, putting a loop around the horse's muzzle. Pressure on the tender flesh above the nostrils with the rope brought the horse into hand.

At the snubbing post, Brian used his bandana to blindfold Snapper. The horse stood quivering, but not trying to fight. Brian worked a hackamore onto its head and snubbed it to the post.

He was breathing hard, limping some, as he went to fetch his saddle. From the corner of an eye, he glanced at Laurie and Hunt. They were perched on the operyhouse rail, ready to watch him ride. They leaned their heads close together. Hunt whispered something. Laurie laughed lightly, as if it had been a good joke.

Brian flung the saddle across Snapper's withers, settling it into place. Then he jammed a knee roughly into Snapper's side and jerked up the cinches. His thoughts were all on Hunt and the girl and the little private jokes that he suspected were about him.

Jump asked him, "You want me to ear for you?"

He shook his head. He didn't want Jump's help. He didn't want any help. He didn't want to need help. This wasn't a raw bronc. It had been ridden before. If he was the man he counted himself to be, he could handle Snapper alone.

Loosing the horse from the snubbing post, he caught the heel knot of the hackamore and pulled Snapper's head around. Snapper turned at the pull, moving cautiously because of the blindfold. Brian maneuvered the horse until its off side was against the snubbing post and it couldn't shift its body away from him. He kept pulling the hackamore until Snapper's muzzle was around almost to the saddle. Holding the bosal tight, he got a foot into the nigh stirrup.

He knew he might be playing the fool, letting his pride get the best of him. The ranch work should come first, and there were better ways to handle a green horse. Ways less likely to injure the horse or the rider. The horse should be sacked out first, reminded of the saddles it had worn in the past, and reassured that the rider meant it no harm. It should at least be treated gently.

Brian knew he was being rougher than he should. He was upsetting the horse. He was taking a chance by not having one of the boys hold Snapper for him until he could get his seat set in the saddle and his boots in the stirrups. But the embarrassed anger in him was too strong to be ignored. It drove him. And, hell, he had handled green broncs by himself before.

Swinging to the saddle, he let go the bosal and whipped away the blindfold.

Snapper snatched rein before he could firm his grip. Inches of mccarty burned through his gloved hand, and the horse's head jerked down between its forelegs. At the same time, its rump went up, heels shooting out.

Brian was pitched forward. His legs grabbed tight to the saddle. His left foot was in the stirrup but his right wasn't. It groped. The horse's sudden buck flung the loose stirrup out, then snapped it back against his knee. The strain on his thighs was making his bruised leg hurt. It didn't want to stay clamped to the saddle. He knew he was very close to coming loose. He fought to stay put.

Snapper caught the ground under all four hoofs and instantly went up again. Brian still didn't have the off stirrup. His rump cleared the saddle. He was aware that a shameful amount of daylight showed under him. He could hear mocking hoots and calls from the opery gallery.

As he came down, the saddle rose to meet him. It kicked hard against his rump. The jolt ran up his spine, cracking into his skull like a hammer blow.

Snapper went up again. Up and down, up and down, like a walking beam. The horse was bucking hard but straight. Catching the rhythm, Brian got his balance.

112

He found the off stirrup and got his boot set in it. If Snapper kept up the pumphandling, he thought it would be a rough ride but not a hard one to stay with.

Suddenly Snapper changed style. Rolling a shoulder toward the ground, the horse turned out its belly, fishing for the sun.

Brian almost went off. He barely managed to snatch his hooks into the cinch and hold himself to the saddle by brute force as the horse dipped.

Snapper came up again, and went down again, twisting to the other side. Over the pounding in his ears, Brian could hear the gallery cheering. He didn't know whether the cheers were for him or the horse. The horse, he reckoned.

The world spun wildly around him as Snapper dipped and twisted. His thigh hurt. His head felt like it was going to snap off his neck and fly away. The sunfishing horse was demanding all the riding skill he had. But bedamned if he'd let the horse get the best of him. Not while that bunch was watching.

Suddenly Snapper stopped sunfishing and started to swap ends. The jolt of the change almost unglued Brian. He almost grabbed the horn. Almost shamed himself by hanging on with his hands. But despite the pain in his thigh, his legs stayed clamped to Snapper's sides. His seat stayed close to the saddle.

Even as he silently cursed the horse, he admired it. This was one hell of a bronc. Damned few horses would have so many tricks in their bag. Some might try to slap a man off by hammering the saddle at his spine. Some would try to spin him loose. Snapper was working at both, weaving and windmilling, high rolling and pumphandling. By the time Brian could get set into one style, the horse would fling itself into something else.

But Brian was every bit as determined as Snapper. He meant to stay on that saddle, even if he had to use his gut hooks in the cinch to do it. Only, as Snapper suddenly swung back into a fit of sunfishing, Brian felt the saddle shift. Something snapped. He still had his seat close to leather, but he was being flung out to the end of the mccarty. He was leaving the horse. The saddle was going with him. It had come loose. And there wasn't one damned thing he could do now but fall.

He slammed into the ground with the saddle still between his legs. His shoulder hit first. His spine corkscrewed as his legs tried to go over his head. For an instant, he felt as if he were being wrenched apart at the joints.

Then he was face down in the mud with his legs tangled in the saddle and recollections of man-stomping broncs vivid in his mind.

Shoving an elbow, he rolled himself onto his back. At the same time, he was trying to kick loose of the saddle. The sounds around him were a turmoil of shouting and hoofs slapping mud. Mud caked his face. Forcing up his eyelids, he squinted through his lashes.

He saw Snapper rearing over him, dark and violent as a tornado against a gray sky. He saw the fresh-shod hoofs flashing out.

A rope shot toward Snapper like a streak of lightning. The loop jerked closed on the horse's hoofs. Snapper half spun, dancing upright, awkward as a Gypsy's bear.

Another rope came from a different direction. It dropped over Snapper's head. As it tightened, the horse fell.

Jump and Eddie held Snapper on the ground, strung out between them.

Catching breath, Brian slowly pulled one boot out of the tangle of saddle rigging. His thigh hurt like hell. His whole body hurt. Silent curses ran through his head. He freed the other boot, then shoved himself to a sitting position.

Hands reached to help him. Laurie's voice came from close beside him. "Oh, Brian! Are you hurt?"

"Unh-unh," he grunted, scrubbing at the mud on his face. "You got a wipe?"

She thrust a bandana into his hand.

He worked the mud away from his eyes with it and looked at her. She sure as hell was a pretty little thing with those big dark eyes all worried over him. Her mouth was puckered with concern. It looked ripe for kissing.

Beyond her, he saw Hunt still perched on the opery rail. Hunt's frown seemed disappointed.

"Are you sure you're all right?" Laurie asked Brian.

He felt tempted to admit that he hurt all over. He would have liked to let her tend and comfort him. But he sure couldn't do a thing like that in front of Hunt and the boys. Dragging himself to his feet, he said gruffly, "I'm all right."

His bones felt like they had come unbolted and were running askew at the joints. His whole body felt thoroughly battered. He would have more than one damned sore bruise come morning, he thought as he tried his legs. Stiffly, he bent from the waist and tugged at his saddle. He flopped it over and spread the rigging to examine it.

The clinches were whole. The latigos were sound and lashed tight through the rigging rings. On the near side the leathers that held the rigging rings to the saddle were fine. The reinforcing patches Laurie had laced onto them were snug and secure.

On the other side, the rings were tied tight to the cinches. But they were free of the saddle leathers. He fingered the edge of a leather. It was torn through where the rings had rubbed it. This was the point he had told Laurie to reinforce. The holes she had punched to lace the patch on were there. A piece of thong still hung in one hole. The patch and the rest of the lacing were gone. Both of the offside leathers had lost their patches. Both had torn through where the rigging rings had chafed them.

That shouldn't have happened, Brian thought. Not if Laurie had done her job right. The sudden anger in him was as fierce as the pain. Laurie was standing by his side, gazing at the muddy saddle. He wheeled to face her. "What the hell did you have in mind? Getting my neck busted for me?"

She jerked back at the blast of his anger.

Jump and Eddie were still holding Snapper down. Jump called, "What's the matter?"

"Come look!" Brian shouted back.

Hunt caught Brian's tone to Laurie if not the words. Dropping from the corral rail, he strode over and glared at Brian. "What did you just say to Miss Laurie?"

"That's none of your damned business!" Brian said.

Hunt's eyes narrowed, offering battle. "Anything that bothers Miss Laurie is my business."

Jump and Eddie loosed Snapper and rode up to Brian. Jump slid from his horse to hunker and examine the saddle. He fingered the torn leathers, then looked up at his sister. "It came loose. Where you patched it, it came loose."

"It couldn't!" she protested.

"You never finished the job," Brian said to her. He gave a jerk of his head at Hunt. "You were working on it when *he* showed up. You left the job and never went back and finished it."

"I did not!"

"Exactly what are you accusing Miss Laurie of?" Hunt demanded.

"Carelessness," Brian snapped back at him. "Unless she did it on purpose to get my neck broke!"

Jump grabbed Brian's sleeve. "Don't you say that! Don't you say such things about my sister!"

Brian glared at him. "Maybe *you* done it! You've had it in for me since I came here. You've meant to get my scalp ever since I set you down with my fist. Maybe you undone the work she did!"

"No!" Laurie screeched at him. "Jump would never do such a thing!"

Hunt dropped a heavy hand on Brian's shoulder. "Mister, you've got no business talking to these good people like that. You'll apologize! You understand me?"

Brian felt the urge to wheel and slam a fist into Hunt's face. But his bones ached from his fall. His legs almost wobbled under him. He was afraid that at this moment even Eddie could knock him over with the shove of a little finger. It was no time to try fighting Hunt. Swallowing at his anger, he jerked away from Hunt and scooped up the saddle.

Hunt grabbed at him again. "You'll apologize to them or you'll answer to me!"

"I'll get my own damned apologies out of him!" Jump shouted.

"Stop it!" Laurie screeched. "Everybody stop it! Can't you — he — I —" Her voice broke. She caught Hunt's hand, pulling him away from Brian. Her eyes were flooding with tears. She pressed her face to Hunt's shoulder.

As Hunt turned his attention to comforting her, he darted a very smug, satisfied look at Brian.

With a grunt of disgust, Brian hefted the saddle to his back and strode out of the corral. Legs aching and awkward, he headed for the shed.

"What about the horses, Mister Brian?" Eddie called after him. The boy's voice was full of disappointment. He was eager to start riding his string. "Ain't we gonna saddle no more?"

"Not right now," Brian answered without looking back.

118

Scornfully, Hunt shouted at him, "Don't worry about the bronc that dumped you, cowboy! I'll take the kinks out of him for you!"

That was a biting insult. It brought Brian up short. He shouted back, "Like hell you will! That horse is in *my* string! *I* ride him!"

"I'll relieve you of the responsibility." Hunt's voice curled at the edges, sarcastically mocking. "I'll buy him off Sam and you won't have to see him again!"

"Like hell!" Brian repeated. The horse was in his string now. It might belong to Sam Pearson but in every other way, it was Brian's. He had the right to say whether anyone else rode it, or whether it was sold off the string. He had the right to quit the ranch if the owner sold it from under him, or even loaned it without his leave. And he damned well meant to make a using horse out of Snapper before he left the Forked P. He meant to put it through its paces in front of Frank Hunt by the time the roundup was over.

Hildy had heard the shouting. She came out onto the stoop of the cabin and peered at Brian as he headed for the shed.

"Is something wrong, Brian?" she called. "Has someone been hurt?"

"No, ma'am!" he replied, his voice still sharp with anger. "No, everything's just fine!"

CHAPTER
TEN

There was a lot of work to be done and not much time to do it in. Despite the aches and the anger, Brian knew he had to have the outfit ready for roundup. He couldn't waste the day humouring himself. After a short rest and a talk with Hildy over a cup of coffee, he headed back to work.

He had left his saddle on the bench outside the shed. This time he meant to repair it himself, and know it was done right. He went on into the shed for tools.

The top of the workbench inside the shed was littered with punches and awls, knives and files. Scraps of cut leather lay around. It was easy to see that Laurie had walked off without cleaning up. Easy to figure she had left before finishing the job she had started.

A dirt-grimed glass window over the workbench gave enough dim light for crude work. He cut thongs and reinforcing strips there, then took them outside. Sitting astride the bench by the door, he pulled the saddle to him. With the off side up, he lifted the fender and looked closely at the broken rigging. There was a lot of mud on it. He wiped the mud away with his bandana. The leathers were worn very thin where they were torn through.

120

As he fingered one, he thought back to his long ride over Ade's Ridge. He had checked out the saddle each day before he put it on his horse. He had kept a close eye on the wear, knowing his life might depend on the soundness of the rigging. The leathers had been worn then but he was sure they hadn't been ready to let go yet when he gave the saddle to Laurie for repair.

He went into the shed again, found a candle in a tin holder on a shelf, and lit it. He held the open flame close to the surface of the workbench. By the flickering light, he studied the dust on the bench. Licking a fingertip, he touched it to one small pile of dust. He held the finger close to the flame as he peered at it. Then he went outside and looked at it by daylight. Finally, he tasted it. There was no doubt that it was leather dust. Returning to the workbench, he began to examine the files. He found a rattail with flecks of leather dust still in the teeth.

That didn't prove someone had used the file on his saddle leathers. But it sure looked to him like the leathers had been filed almost to the breaking point. If the patches had been laced loosely into place and the laces left unknotted, the job would have looked all right, but would have let go under strain. Some time during the saddling of the winter-snuffy horses, the whole rig was sure to let loose.

Somebody had intended for Brian to get dumped, maybe stomped, maybe killed.

Laurie had worked on the saddle, and she had been mad at him, but he couldn't believe she would pull a trick like that on him.

Jump had sworn to get even with him. Maybe a hot-headed kid could do such a thing, but Jump had a streak of pride that suggested he would sooner face an enemy than go sneaking around pulling coyote tricks.

Then there was Frank Hunt. Hunt had been hanging around a hell of a lot. He would have had an opportunity to get at the saddle. Did he have a reason? Brian knew Hunt didn't like him. Was that reason enough? Or was there more?

Somebody had burned down the Pearson's barn. Somebody had slaughtered the Pearson's prize bull. Had that same somebody tried to wipe out Pearson's hired hand too? Was it all Frank Hunt's doing? Would Hunt try to destroy the father while he was courting the daughter?

Brian decided it was time to have a long talk with Frank Hunt.

Jump and Eddie were still at the corral. They told him Hunt had left while he was in the cabin with Hildy. Brian stopped at the cabin long enough to strap on his gunbelt and borrow Sam's saddle. He threw the saddle onto one of the using horses and set out looking for Hunt's tracks.

He picked them up easily. They crossed the meadow and turned onto a well-worn trail. Riding the trail, Brian scanned the land ahead for sight of Hunt. But this land was too rough, too patched with woods and broken with outcrops of rock. He could never see far up the trail.

Judging from the sign, Hunt was holding a steady trot. Brian kept to the same gait. He didn't want to push his horse hard on the rough trail. And his bones ached. Damn, they ached.

He had ridden some distance when the sudden sound of gunshots startled him.

Three shots far off to his left. Two more shots. And three more. Two different guns, he thought. It sounded like an exchange of gunfire. A couple of people shooting at each other.

He swung off the trail. As he rode in the direction of the gunfire, he heard one more shot. The sound faded slowly, as if the gun had been fired within a canyon where the walls rebounded an echo.

He passed beyond the range he had ridden with Jump and Bailey. This was strange land to him. He had heard of canyons over this way. A Wolf Canyon and one called Bad Water Canyon. None of the ranchers ran stock near them in the winter. They weren't safe range for spring calves.

He spotted fresh droppings on a game trail that crossed ahead of him. Droppings from a grain-fed horse. A few marks of shod hoofs told him the horse had a rider on its back. It had gone in the direction he was heading no more than an hour ago.

The game trail took him upslope, winding through land that grew steadily rougher. Then it cut through a tangle of scrubby woods. The trees petered out on rocky ground. Ahead of him, Brian saw the mouth of a canyon.

The canyon was a deep cut in a sharp ridge. Its walls were steep but ragged with ledges, nooks, and cracks that would make fine dens for wolves and snakes. There was brush growing in the muddy bottoms of the canyon and on some of the ledges.

Halting at the gap, Brian looked into the canyon and sniffed the slight breeze that came through it. The ground told him nothing. The spring thaws had made it too sloppy to hold prints. The breeze brought the scents of wolves, of droppings, of dead meat and old dens.

And silence. The canyon was very quiet. No insects chittered. No birds called. Nothing stirred. Something had spooked the wild things that lived there.

He drew his revolver as he lifted rein to ride on into the mouth of the canyon.

Suddenly he heard a horse behind him. It broke into a gallop. Wheeling, he looked back. The horse had been some distance behind him. And it was leaving in a hurry. He barely glimpsed motion before it was gone from sight.

Evidently the rider ahead of him on the trail had seen or heard him coming and had taken to cover. Once Brian was well past, the rider had bolted.

Was it Frank Hunt? he wondered.

He started to spur his mount, meaning to race after the unseen rider. As his rowels touched the horse's flanks, lead sung past his head. The sound of the shot rattled around in the canyon like the rumble of thunder.

A *trap*, Brian thought as he threw himself out of the saddle. He dropped to the far side of his horse, away from the source of the shot. Hanging on to the reins with his left hand, he kept the horse's body between himself and whoever had fired at him.

Over his shoulder, he glanced at the trail, expecting to see the rider returning. But the sound of hoofs had faded. He looked into the canyon again.

The bullet had come from a height well above his head and just inside the mouth of the canyon. From one of the ledges to his left. He held his revolver pointed across his saddle, aiming in the general direction of the ledges. Peering over the sights, he studied the ledges.

There!

He spotted something sticking out of a bush on one ledge. It looked like the muzzle of a long gun. He set his sights on it. The hammer under his thumb was back at full cock. His forefinger was tense on the trigger. But he didn't want to go shooting somebody, especially when he didn't know who it was.

"Hold on, mister!" he shouted. "I got a bead on you!"

The gun muzzle in the brush wavered. It drooped. Sliding from the brush, the rifle clattered down the rocks. The bush trembled, then was still.

Puzzled, Brian waited a long moment. Nothing happened. Cautiously, he nudged his horse into motion. He kept its body between himself and the ledge as he worked toward the fallen gun. Ducking under the horse's belly, he grabbed it.

It was an old Spencer, its weathered stock studded with brass tacks. There was a live round under the uncocked hammer. A pair of feathers dangled from the trigger guard. Fingering the feathers, he wondered if that was an Indian up there in the brush.

Something stirred on the ledge. Backstepping, Brian saw a sleek gray head. Pointed ears were held flat back to it. A wolf skulked along the ledge. He could see no other motion. No sign of the man on the ledge trying to escape the wolf. Maybe the man was injured, he thought. Maybe he'd passed out. Or died. Maybe the scent of blood was drawing the wolf.

Brian kept backing until he had the bulk of the wolf's body in view. Lifting the Spencer, he set the sights just behind the shoulder and squeezed the trigger.

The wolf leaped back, crouching in surprise. The slug had missed. The old Spencer threw low and to the left. Compensating as he resighted, Brian fired again.

The wolf slammed back against the canyon wall. It staggered, thrashing, then stumbled off the ledge. As it tumbled down the rock face of the canyon, it went limp. Brian was certain it was already dead when it hit bottom, crashing into a thicket of brush.

The man in the bushes on the ledge never stirred.

He had to be unconscious or dead, Brian decided. And alone. Groundhitching his horse, he chose a way up to the ledge. He carried the Spencer with him as he began to climb.

He found the Indian lying belly down with one arm stretched out into the brush. There was a lot of blood on the back of the Indian's hide shirt, and more on one of his blanket leggings. He looked like he might be dead.

Keeping the Spencer cautiously pointed at the Indian, Brian moved closer. The man's face was turned toward him. He thought he recognized it. This looked like one of the men who had ridden to Pearson's ranch with Bent Knee.

The Indian's eyelids fluttered. Brian saw one arm tense. The Indian was alive. Conscious. And collecting himself to try an attack.

Warily, Brian kept the rifle aimed at the Indian as he backstepped. He said, "Look here, *I* ain't the one who shot you. You know that, don't you?"

The Indian showed no reaction.

"You need help. I'll give you a hand." Brian was afraid the Indian didn't understand him. It was a hell of a world where men didn't all use the same words. It made for a lot of trouble. Hoping he could make himself clear, he lowered the gun muzzle. With his empty hand, he pointed to himself. "Friend. Remember? Pearson's friend. Friend to Bent Knee."

The Indian's lashes flicked as he peered at Brian from under them.

"Friend," Brian insisted, pointing to himself, then to the Indian and back again. "Give beef to Bent Knee. Remember? Give help to Indian. Savvy?"

He thought maybe the Indian was getting his drift. Maybe it didn't matter. The Indian looked too badly hurt to be dangerous. He didn't look like he'd be able to stay conscious much longer. Brian started to move closer.

The whinny of a horse startled hell out of him.

His own horse answered.

Wheeling, he looked out from the ledge.

There were three Indians on horseback just beyond the mouth of the canyon. One was leading a riderless horse with feathers braided in its mane. All of them had rifles pointed at Brian.

Very slowly, very cautiously, Brian set down the Spencer. Facing the Indians below, he lifted his hands high and clear to show them empty.

One Indian stepped his horse up into the mouth of the canyon. Brian recognized him as Bent Knee. The others stayed where they were.

"Friend!" Brian called out to Bent Knee. "Pearson's friend! Remember?"

Bent Knee's face was set cold and hard. There was no trace of friendship in it. He gestured for Brian to come down.

Leaving the Spencer on the ledge, Brian climbed to the canyon floor. As he faced Bent Knee, he waved at the ledge. "One of your men is up there. He's been shot. Hurt bad from the look of him. He needs help. I was trying to help him."

Bent Knee gave Brian no reply, but called out in his own language to the men behind him. One dismounted and approached Bent Knee.

Bent Knee spoke again.

The Indian he had called started up to the ledge. Bent Knee watched him in silence. Brian watched, feeling a dark chill along his spine. He hoped the man up there was still alive.

The Indian reached the ledge and called out to Bent Knee.

Bent Knee looked at Brian. "You shoot Stone Knife?"

"Hell no! I heard the shooting and come to see what was going on. I found him up there. He took a shot at me before he passed out. There was a wolf after him. I shot the wolf to keep it from getting him."

The Indian who had climbed to the ledge called out again. He sounded excited. Angry. Brian wished to hell he could understand what the man was saying.

Bent Knee snapped a reply back to the Indian, then looked down his gun barrel at Brian. He seemed about to trigger the gun full into Brian's face.

"White man come go shoot Indian. Indian come go shoot white man," he said, his tone very reasonable, as if he expected Brian to see the sense of what he said and to agree with him that it would all even out.

"No sir!" Brian protested. "The white man you want is the one who shot him. You don't want to shoot just any old white man you happen to come across. That ain't right! Dammit, I was trying to help him!"

"Why you help?" Bent Knee asked.

"Because he's hurt and he needs help. You'd stop to help a white man if you found him shot up, wouldn't you?" Brian said.

Bent Knee looked uncertain.

"You ought to be trying to help him now yourself instead of standing around palavering. If he don't get patched up right quick he's going to die."

Bent Knee frowned slightly, puzzling over the flow of Brian's words. He seemed to get the gist of them. His hand on the gun eased as he called out to the man he had sent up onto the ledge. The man replied. Then Bent Knee spoke to the one who had stayed with the horses. That one said something and slid down from his mount. He tied all three horses and started away afoot.

Bent Knee spoke to Brian again. "You no come go shoot Stone Knife?"

"Hell no! It wasn't me who done it!"

"Who?"

"I don't know. I didn't get a look at him. Didn't you see any other white men around here?"

"No."

"What about the others? They see anybody?"

Bent Knee frowned, not understanding.

"Were you all riding together?" Brian asked. Moving tentatively, he brought down his hands. Bent Knee didn't object. Still cautious, Brian began to make signs. He indicated four riders traveling together, question, four riders traveling separately. At the same time, he said, "You. Them. Other Indians. Ride together. Yes? No?"

Bent Knee understood that. "Bent Knee hunt meat. Much Talk hunt meat. Yellow Face hunt meat. Stone Knife hunt meat. One. One. One. One."

So they had all been hunting sign of game separately. Brian suggested, "Maybe one of the others seen a white man while you were apart."

"Stone Knife see white man," Bent Knee said in a tone of agreement. "White man shoot Stone Knife."

"What makes you so sure it was a white man? Maybe an Indian shot him."

"No Indian. Indian camp much far. No Indian this place here. Bent Knee no shoot. Much Talk no shoot. Yellow Face no shoot."

So if there were no Indians around except the hunting party and none of them had done the shooting, it had to have been a white man who did it.

Brian asked, "You know Frank Hunt?"

Bent Knee's frown told him the name wasn't familiar.

Pointing south, Brian explained. "A rancher from down yonder. The Rocking H brand." He sketched the brand in the air with his forefinger.

Bent Knee nodded with comprehension. "Soldier-No-Soldier."

Hunt had been an Army officer, but no longer was. Brian said, "Yeah, him. Frank Hunt."

"Soldier-No-Soldier no friend. No come go give beef to Indian. Indian no more come go see Soldier-No-Soldier. Him make shoot, say kill Indian. No friend. Him white man shoot Stone Knife?"

"I don't know. He was around these parts. I was following after him when I heard the shooting. I was hoping maybe one of you seen him."

Bent Knee called out to the man still waiting on the ledge. As the man replied, the third Indian returned. He was dragging a handful of long poles with him. He dropped them near the horses, chose a horse, and began to rig a travois.

Bent Knee spoke to him. He paused in his work and answered with much gesturing. When he finished talking, Bent Knee told Brian, "Yellow Face see white man. No Soldier-No-Soldier. White man Beef-Killer. Ride fast. Come go." He pointed south.

"Beef-Killer?"

"White man no friend. Kill much beef. No eat. No come go give Indian. Coyote eat much beef. Indian hungry. Beef-Killer no friend."

"You mean somebody killed a mess of cattle and left it to the coyotes?"

"Kill much big beef. Shoot. No sick beef. Good beef. No eat."

"Wait a minute! You mean that somebody shot a big beef? A big red bull?"

"No bull. Beef. Wohaw."

Bent Knee thought by the word *bull* Brian meant a buffalo. Brian tried to make himself clear. "Was it a big he-beef? A he-wohaw? A big red he-beef with a forked P burnt on its hide?"

"He-beef," Bent Knee agreed. "Much big red he-beef. Pearson beef. Beef-Killer no come go give Indian beef."

"This was out yonder a good ways?" Brian gestured in the direction that he had found the dead Durham.

Bent Knee nodded.

"And you seen who shot it?"

"Stone Knife see Beef-Killer shoot beef. Stone Knife come go take beef. Beef-Killer make shoot Stone Knife. Stone Knife come go say Bent Knee. Bent Knee come go get take beef. Beef-Killer make shoot Bent Knee. Indians go away. Sun come go." Bent Knee pointed at the sky and swung his arm, indicating the travel of the sun. "Indian come go see beef. No more good. Beef too much dead. Coyotes eat. No good Indian come go eat. No good!"

As Brian understood it, the Indians had seen a man shoot the Durham and had tried to take the carcass but the man had run them off. They returned later, but by then it was too late. The bull had been dead too long. The coyotes had been at it, and it was no longer fit to eat. Bent Knee was right riled by the whole affair, especially the waste of good meat.

Brian felt right riled himself. He said, "Yellow Face seen the same Beef-Killer somewhere around here just now?"

Nodding, Bent Knee spoke to the man who was putting together the travois. Yellow Face paused. He gestured at Brian as he replied. He kept talking as he returned to work. When he finished the travois, he walked over to Bent Knee. He made more gestures at Brian. He was still talking.

His voice was loud and demanding. His speech seemed much too long to be simply a reply to Brian's question. And his gestures didn't look friendly at all.

At last he finished what he was saying. Bent Knee spoke tersely to him. With a shrug that looked disgusted, he turned away. He started up to the ledge where Much Talk and Stone Knife waited.

Bent Knee turned to Brian. "Yellow Face see Beef-Killer make ride this place. You say Beef-Killer shoot Stone Knife?"

"Maybe. I don't know. I didn't see. I can't say for sure. But it seems likely to me."

"Yellow Face say Bent Knee make come go shoot Beef-Killer. Say Bent Knee come go shoot you. Say shoot much white man. Say come go take much beef. Indian come go eat much. No hungry."

"That wouldn't do you no good and you know it," Brian protested. "You go around shooting up a lot of people and stealing the beef, and you'd just get the soldiers out here hunting you. They'd shoot you and Yellow Face and all your women and young'uns too."

Bent Knee gave a sad nod. "Soldiers no friend Indian."

The men on the ledge were coming down, carrying Stone Knife with them. Stone Knife was unconscious. Once they were down, they secured him to the travois.

Bent Knee spoke to Brian again. "You come go Indian camp."

"I got to get back to the ranch," Brian said. "I got a lot of work to do."

"You come go Indian camp," Bent Knee repeated. This time he made it clear he wasn't offering an invitation, but giving an order.

"I can't go," Brian protested.

Suddenly Bent Knee's rifle was pointing into Brian's face again. Bent Knee's eyes darted to Brian's gunbelt. "Come go give Bent Knee gun."

Brian felt a wince in his gut. He realized he hadn't convinced the Indians that he wasn't the one who shot Stone Knife. Bent Knee might be willing to listen to reason, but he wasn't going to let a possible Indian-killer go loose. The rifle aimed at Brian's face couldn't be argued with.

Reluctantly, Brian unstrapped the gunbelt and held it out. As Bent Knee took it from him, he said, "That ain't no present, mind you. I want it back. Savvy?"

"Good gun?" Bent Knee asked. He closed the buckle and slung the looped gunbelt over his shoulder.

Brian nodded, hoping Bent Knee wasn't the kind who would kill a man just for a gun. "I paid a good piece of money for it. I worked hard to earn the money. I want the gun back. You be careful with it. Savvy?"

Bent Knee seemed almost to smile. He said, "Dead man no need gun."

"Dammit, I didn't shoot Stone Knife!"

"Maybe no," Bent Knee allowed. He waved at Brian's horse, indicating that he wanted Brian to mount up. "You come go Indian camp. You friend, no make rope hands. No hurt. Yes? Maybe you no friend. Maybe all talk no true. You no friend, you die."

That was clear enough. Either Brian went along with them peaceably or he would be tied up and hauled along. Either he proved to be telling the truth about Stone Knife or he would be killed.

One wrong move and likely he'd be killed anyway, he thought darkly as he collected his horse and stepped to the saddle. He reined over to the travois and looked at Stone Knife. The Indian's face was greenish pale and his breathing thinly shallow. As Bent Knee came alongside, Brian asked, "How far is it to your camp?"

"Much far," Bent Knee said. "Come go camp, come go sun."

Brian wasn't sure whether he meant that they would reach the camp after nightfall, or after a full day's travel. Either way, it was too far. Stone Knife didn't look like he could last through a long jolting ride overland on the travois.

Brian didn't want to see the man die. He damned well didn't want Stone Knife to die without waking and telling the others it wasn't Brian who shot him.

Bent Knee seemed like a decent sort, he thought. Hildy said her husband was right fond of Bent Knee and his people. She said it in a kindly way as if she shared the feeling. And Bent Knee evidently respected the Pearsons.

"You better take Stone Knife to the Pearsons'," Brian told Bent Knee. He hoped to hell his judgment was sound. He wouldn't want to put the Pearsons into danger. But it seemed like the only hope of keeping Stone Knife alive.

Bent Knee looked at him in question.

"He's lost a lot of blood." Brian spoke slowly, wanting to be sure Bent Knee understood. "He won't last out a long trip. The Pearson ranch is a lot closer than your camp. You'd better take him there. Missus Pearson can doctor him. She can do as good a job as a medicine man. She's got stuff there at the ranch to fix up wounds and ease pain."

Bent Knee didn't answer. Face thoughtful, he rode on. Brian kept pace at his side, waiting for a reply. The others followed. After a moment, Bent Knee said, "You say woman Pearson make medicine for Stone Knife?"

"Damned good medicine. The same kind she uses on Pearson," Brian told him.

He looked over his shoulder at Yellow Face and Much Talk. After another moment of thought, he spoke to them. Yellow Face answered sharply, objecting. Bent

136

Knee drew rein. The others moved up close and began to talk with him.

Listening to their tone, Brian decided they were arguing, and not getting anywhere. He interrupted them. "You're wasting time. Stone Knife is hurt too bad to keep hanging on while you jaw all day. You'd better get him to Missus Pearson quick if you don't want him to die."

Bent Knee looked askance at him.

"Die soon!" Brian said, waving a hand at Stone Knife. "Need help. Missus Pearson make help. You savvy?"

Slowly, Bent Knee nodded. He spoke to the others again, this time with an air of command. Lifting rein, he headed his mount toward the Pearson ranch.

CHAPTER
ELEVEN

Bent Knee drew rein on the ridge overlooking the Pearson ranch. Brian stopped at his side. The others halted behind him. Bent Knee scanned the yard and the meadows and the slopes beyond.

"Damn!" Brian grunted as he looked down at the corrals.

Bent Knee glanced at him in question.

"I told them not to do that," Brian said. In the breaking corral, Jump had saddled a horse and was astride it. The horse was jacking around, alternating crowhops and high kicks while Jump fanned it with his hat. Eddie and Laurie were standing by on using horses, ready with their ropes in case anything went wrong.

It didn't look like anything would go wrong. The horse wasn't wild, just frisky. Jump was handling it well. The boy really could ride, Brian thought. Even so, he was angry at being disobeyed. Jump shouldn't be topping a bronc without him around to be sure everything was safe.

"No see no bad," Bent Knee said. It was part comment, part question. He couldn't spot signs of

138

trouble, and he was concerned that Brian saw something he didn't.

Brian realized Bent Knee didn't care about the boy on the bronc, but only about possible danger to himself and his companions. He told Bent Knee, "It looks all right to me."

Nodding, Bent Knee urged his horse on down the slope toward the yard. Brian and the others followed.

The hound spotted them first. It had been lying on the stoop sunning itself. It lifted its head and sniffed the air. Catching scent, it rose and gave a bark. A call of warning to its people.

Eddie saw the riders. Waving an arm toward them, he shouted, "Look!"

Jump heard him and looked. The distraction cost Jump his seat. Suddenly he was up at the end of his reins and the horse was hopping out from under him. As he hit the ground, Laurie was spinning out her rope. Her loop dropped over the horse's head. But this horse had no intention of going back to stomp the fallen rider. Rid of the weight, it came to a settled halt.

Eddie hesitated just long enough to be sure that Jump and Laurie didn't need his help. Then he hightailed for the cabin, shouting for Hildy. She heard him and came onto the stoop. He pointed at the approaching riders. Squinting, she peered toward them.

Brian cupped his hands to his mouth and called out, "Hallo the house!"

"Brian!" Hildy shouted back. "Is that Bent Knee with you?"

"Yes, ma'am! We've got a bad hurt man here. He needs help. I was hoping you'd doctor him up."

"Bring him on in!"

As Brian and the Indians rode into the yard, Jump piled over the corral fence and raced toward the cabin. Laurie hurried after him. He disappeared inside the cabin. She halted at the stoop with her mother and Eddie.

Suddenly Jump came bursting from the cabin with a rifle in his hands.

Brian sensed Bent Knee's start at the sight of the gun. With a gesture for the Indians not to worry, he snapped at Jump, "Boy, you set that gun down! We don't want any trouble!"

Jump began to protest. Hildy interrupted him, speaking softly but firmly. He didn't answer her, but backed into the cabin.

Brian was pretty sure Jump wasn't putting the gun away, only putting himself and it out of sight. He hoped the damnfool kid wouldn't go off half-cocked.

Hildy stood on the stoop with Laurie at one side and Eddie at the other. The hound waited restlessly at their feet. Nudging his mother, Eddie pointed and said in a very loud whisper, "Ma, look! Bent Knee's got Mister Brian's gun!"

Hildy touched Eddie with a hand meant to silence him. She questioned Brian with her eyes.

"It's all right, ma'am," he said, reining up in front of her. "There ain't any trouble. Just a hurt man who needs help."

Laurie was gazing at him with concern. "Are you all right?"

The way she asked gave him a warm feeling. Despite the tension in him, he grinned as he nodded in reply.

Hildy went to look at the man on the travois. She called anxiously to Laurie, "Go inside and lay a pallet. Put it in the bedroom next to your Pa."

"You gonna let them into the house?" Eddie asked, surprised at the idea.

"This man is hurt bad," Hildy told him. Then she looked at Bent Knee and smiled. It was a taut smile, but a sincere one. "Step down and bring your hurt friend on inside, Bent Knee. I'll see what I can do for him."

Bent Knee slid off his horse and walked over to her. He limped slightly. Holding out a hand to her, he said, "You make medicine. Make good Stone Knife. Much friend."

"Of course I'll help. I'll do everything I can." She shook the hand. "Just bring him on inside."

Bent Knee spoke to Yellow Face and Much Talk. They dismounted and unlashed Stone Knife from the travois. Carrying him between them, they followed Hildy into the cabin.

"I'll take care of the horses," Brian said, stepping down from his saddle.

"No! You stay Bent Knee." It was an order. Bent Knee made it clear that he considered Brian a hostage.

Eddie was standing with one hand on the head of the hound that was pressed up against his legs. He gazed at Brian, looking almost as worried as the dog did.

"Eddie" — Brian kept his voice calm and casual — "how about you look after these horses while Bent Knee and me see to Stone Knife?"

Eddie wasn't sure whether to be afraid or thrilled by the Indians' visit. The confidence in Brian's manner gave him some assurance. But the fact that Brian's gunbelt was on Bent Knee's shoulder worried him. He nodded solemnly.

Brian grinned at him.

He grinned back. As he started for the horses, he asked curiously, "Is that the hurt one's name? Stone Knife?"

"Uh-huh."

"What happened to him?"

"Somebody shot him."

"Who?"

Brian shrugged as he handed the boy his reins. "Maybe the Beef-Killer."

Bent Knee glared suspiciously as Eddie reached for his reins. Holding onto them, he asked Brian, "What him come go make horses?"

"He's going to put them in the corral. He'll feed and water them," Brian told him.

He looked at the corral, then gave up the horse to Eddie.

"Who's the Beef-Killer?" Eddie asked.

"That's something I'd sure like to know," Brian said as he started up the steps.

Bent Knee followed him into the cabin. Hildy had led the other Indians into the bedroom. Jump was alone in the living room, standing by the fireplace. He looked tight-strung and angry. He had put away the rifle but he'd gotten himself a revolver. It was tucked into his waistband. He had his coat off so that the gunbutt would show. He stood with his gut thrust out, making the gun very obvious. He was trying hard to look powerful and threatening.

The gun was an old Navy Colt, a cap-and-ball revolver that usually had a pin sight. Brian hoped the boy didn't try any fast draw with it. If one of the Indians didn't shoot him while he was trying to tug the gun free of his waistband, he just might have it go off by accident when that pinsight caught in the pants.

Bent Knee scowled at the gun.

Brian said quietly, "Jump, you'd better unload that artillery before you hurt yourself with it."

Jump's face flushed dark red. He darted a look at Brian's gunbelt draped over Bent Knee's shoulder. "At least *I* got a gun! *I* ain't letting anybody take *my* gun away from *me!*"

Bent Knee gave a shake of his head. "Come go give Bent Knee gun."

"No!" Jump's arm twitched as if he were about to go for the gun.

"Easy," Brian said, speaking to the boy and the Indian both. "Nobody wants any trouble."

"I ain't giving up my gun!" Jump replied.

Bent Knee didn't like being defied. He started for Jump. "Bent Knee come go take gun!"

Jump snatched at the Colt.

Brian lunged.

Catching Jump's arm, Brian jerked the boy's hand away from the gun. He wrenched Jump's arm, shoving the boy's back against the wall. His other hand wrapped around the butt of the revolver. His thumb pressed firmly against the hammer, holding it in place against a safety peg. As he tugged the gun, it hung up in Jump's waistband. Jump gave a sudden grunt of pain. The muzzle, maybe the sharp little pin sight, had poked him in the belly. Twisting the gun, Brian gave it another tug. It came free.

"Damn!" Jump shouted as he struggled against Brian's grip "Dammit, whose side are you on?"

"Everybody's side! I don't want anybody getting killed!" Brian breathed between his teeth. The boy was putting up a good fight. It wasn't easy holding him. With the gun finally clear in his hand, he freed Jump's arm. Backstepping, he leveled the revolver at Jump. His thumb rested on the high hammer, but he didn't cock it.

Jump rubbed at the arm Brian had twisted. He glared at Brian. His chest heaved and his Adam's apple jerked. "Damn you! I'll get you!"

Bent Knee held a hand toward Brian. "Come go give gun."

"No," Brian said. "I don't think so. Friends don't go around taking guns away from each other."

Bent Knee looked surprised.

Jump muttered at Brian, "You ain't no friend of mine."

"Bent Knee," Brian said, his tone quiet and reasonable, "you're in *my* camp now. There's womenfolk here I got to look after. If I was to come into your camp among your women, you might want me to give you my gun, but you sure as hell wouldn't want to give me yours. Right?"

Bent Knee thought about it. He didn't look very agreeable.

"You're in my camp now and I ain't asking you to give me your gun," Brian continued. "I'm trusting you and your men. You understand that? *Trust?* You savvy *trust?*"

Bent Knee nodded warily. He looked at Brian, then glanced around the cabin. "No your camp. Pearson camp."

"Pearson's hurt. I'm boss while he's laid up."

"Pearson hurt? Bad hurt?" The news disturbed Bent Knee.

"He'll get well," Brian assured him. "Missus Pearson's making medicine for him. Same as she's doing for Stone Knife. She wouldn't make medicine for Stone Knife if she wasn't a friend to the Indians, would she?"

Bent Knee looked as if he could accept that. But he was spooky on the white man's ground. He wanted to keep the guns, and the upper hand. He gazed at Brian without replying.

"We shake hands. Share food," Brian suggested. "You, me, we be friends. We *trust* each other. You keep your guns and I'll keep mine. Savvy?"

It was hard for Bent Knee to yield. It looked as if it made him ache to slide the gunbelt from his shoulder and set it in Brian's outheld hand. As he did it, he darted a sharp eye at Jump and said. "No give *him* gun. No trust *him.*"

"Damn!" Jump growled.

"Trust *me*," Brian said.

Bent Knee nodded.

"All right. Now I'm going to have a palaver with the boy here." Brian motioned toward Jump. "How about you go in and see how Stone Knife is doing?"

"Stone Knife much hurt. Need much good medicine," Bent Knee muttered as he turned from Brian and stalked into the bedroom.

"Come on outside. I want to talk to you," Brian said to Jump.

Sullenly, the boy followed him into the yard.

The afternoon was aging fast. The sun was slipping down onto the western ridges. There was a chill wind coming from the slopes. Brian shivered slightly at the touch of it. Jump halted at the foot of the steps, his face set hard, as cold and determined as the wind.

The hound had been under the stoop. It came out and rubbed against Jump's legs, whining for reassurance. Keeping his eyes defiantly on Brian, Jump bent enough to scratch the dog's head.

"He ain't any too happy about the Indians, is he?" Brian said.

"First time they came here, he tried to run them," Jump told him. "Pa whupped him. Had to whup him more than once to learn him not to bother them. He ain't been happy about them since."

"Sometimes it takes a couple of whuppings to get a point across," Brian said. He looked up as the door opened.

Much Talk came slowly onto the stoop. He had his rifle in hand. Giving Brian and Jump a wary look, he headed for the corral where the Indian horses were. He stopped and studied them a moment. Satisfied, he seated himself crosslegged on the ground. He set his rifle on his knees. His head drooped as if he dozed. But Brian could sense his steady gaze. Brian guessed that Bent Knee had sent him out to stand guard. And not just over the horses. Much Talk's back was to the horses.

Jump waited silently until the Indian had settled himself. Then he picked up the talk where it had left off. He'd caught Brian's implication. He answered, "I ain't a dog that has to be whupped into a lesson."

"You ain't exactly a growed man who knows what's right without he has to learn it either," Brian told him. "You've been pulling against me like a green colt ever since I came here. I gave you orders not to saddle any of those broncs and first thing my back is turned, you're up on one. You ain't got sense enough to follow orders."

"I got sense enough to follow the ones that are worth following! You give me some dumb old order like I was just a little kid like Eddie, and I ain't going to follow it! We've got to saddle horses if we're going to have them ready for the roundup. You go running off, leave the ranch work that needs doing, somebody's got to do it! We did plenty of work around here before you ever came here. I know the work. I can do it. Only you treat me like I ain't nothing but a little coddling baby that has to have a nursemaid all the time!" All of Jump's angry frustration, all of the pain of trying to grow up and being thwarted in it, ached in his voice.

147

The intensity of Jump's speech took Brian aback. He looked at the boy, remembering when he had been that age himself. He'd been a maverick young'un running half wild. He had begun wrangling when he was no bigger than Eddie. He'd gone up the trail as a nighthawk, riding herd on the remuda each night and driving the cookwagon each day, grabbing sleep in short snatches whenever he had a chance, before he was Jump's age. He had worked together with grown men and they had treated him as one of them. At times, he had been stopped from some foolishness that might have endangered men or the herd. Otherwise, he had been let to make his own mistakes and learn from them.

He wondered how he would have felt if the other hands had tried to look out for him the way he had been looking out for Jump. How would he have felt if someone denied him the right to saddle his own string when he chose? Or had taken his gun away from him, implying he was too young to be allowed a dangerous toy?

He still had Jump's old Navy Colt in his hand. He hefted it. He'd been about Jump's age when he got his first gun, when he first took that power of life and death into his hand. On the trail, on the range, even a boy sometimes needed a gun. A wolf, a rattler, a grizzly, didn't ask your age.

"Jump," he said, "this your gun, or your pa's?"

"Mine."

"Where'd you get it?"

"Pa gave it to me."

148

"When?"

"On my birthday. When I turned fifteen. Almost a year ago."

So Sam Pearson trusted his son not to misuse the gun. Brian asked himself why he felt so certain Jump would do wrong with it. He answered himself that Jump didn't understand the situation with the Indians. And maybe that was as much his own fault as Jump's. Maybe he hadn't given Jump the chance to understand.

"Look here," he said quietly. "These Indians came here as friends. They came because they needed help and I promised it to them. I know I took a chance bringing them, but I figured it was a fair chance. I figured they wouldn't start trouble if we didn't. I figured nobody here would be fool enough to start trouble with them. You understand me?"

Jump nodded, but he looked puzzled.

"I trust these Indians and they trust me," Brian continued. "What I want to know now is whether I can trust you."

"What do you mean?"

"Are you man enough *not* to cause trouble with them? Are you man enough to understand that their ways are different from ours? Can you keep from getting het up about it if they do things wrong, not meaning to, but just because they do things different?"

"Pa already told me they got different ways," Jump said.

"Can you stay friends with them the way your pa can?"

Jump nodded again.

"You think you can carry a gun and still keep peace with them?"

"Uh-huh."

Brian held out the revolver, offering it to Jump.

Jump eyed it suspiciously for a moment before he took it. The hammer rested on a safety peg. He squinted at the caps on the nipples. "You ain't done something to it so it won't shoot?"

"What could I do to it? You've been with me all the time I've had it. Hell, you could do as much damage with an empty gun as a loaded one. The Indians wouldn't know it was empty. If you went for it, they'd shoot first and find that out later."

"No Indian's going to shoot me!" Jump snapped.

"None of them *wants* to! You hear? If they were to up and kill a white man, it'd bring the soldiers down on them. Bent Knee don't want that. Savvy? Do *you* want to shoot one of them? Do you really *want* to?"

"No. Not if I don't have to."

"Well, take my word for it, you don't have to," Brian said. "Jump, you do a fool thing with that gun and it ain't just you who'll suffer. It's your ma and your sister and your pa and Eddie and me, and all the whites and Indians around here."

Jump looked at the gun he held as if he had never seen it before. He looked at it as if he could see through it into the trouble it could make. He looked as if he saw things he had never seen before.

When he lifted his head to face Brian again, the anger was gone from his eyes. They were deep and solemn. There was respect in them, both for Brian and for himself. He understood what it was that Brian had put into his hand. He squared his shoulders against the burden of responsibility he suddenly carried.

"Yes, sir," he said softly.

Brian felt a sense of relief. He felt now that he could trust Jump with the gun. And with more than that. He felt like a war had ended. There would be no more fighting with Jump. From now on, they would work together.

CHAPTER
TWELVE

The glow of early dawn was showing beyond the cabin windows when Brian woke. He realized he had slept long and hard. The air was scented with cooking coffee. Hildy was nowhere to be seen, but Laurie was at the fireplace doing something with the Dutch oven. As he rolled out of his soogans, she glanced at him and smiled.

"Stone Knife still alive?" he asked, collecting a boot and shoving a foot into it.

She nodded. "Ma says he's past the worst of it. She stayed up watching over him all night. She says he should pull through if the wounds don't fester."

"Thank God," he mumbled. He tugged on the other boot. As he hauled himself to his feet, he rediscovered the aches and pains of his fall the day before. Sometimes he wondered if cowboying was worth the hurting. But it was the life he had chosen for himself. Stretching, he tested the soreness in his shoulders. Then he walked over to Laurie's side.

"Where's your ma now?" he asked.

"She went up to rest on my bed a while. I expect she's asleep. She was awful tired," she said.

"I reckon so," he agreed. "Is that coffee ready for drinking yet?"

In reply, she got a cup and poured it full for him. As he took it, she told him, "Brian, Pa's awake. He wants to talk to you."

She looked solemn and concerned, as if she expected Sam to bawl him out. He asked her, "Is he mad at me?"

"I don't know." She didn't meet his eyes.

He thought she did know, and that Sam must be plenty mad. Well, he couldn't blame Sam. He hadn't been doing a hell of a good job handling the ranch work. Not while he'd been fighting Jump and Laurie both. And likely Sam wasn't any too happy about him bringing home the Indians either.

He said, "It ain't easy, you know."

"I know. I guess Jump and I haven't been much help to you. I'm sorry. I didn't understand. Then I saw how your saddle had been messed with so it would come apart. I can't — I didn't do it. And I know Jump would never do a thing like that. All I can figure is maybe Frank did it. I got so mad about the way you hit Jump and all that I kind of — I put Frank up to riling you. But I never thought he'd do a terrible thing like that!" She sounded about to cry.

"I don't think that had anything to do with it," he told her. "I think Frank Hunt wants my hide anyway."

"Why?"

Suddenly he didn't want to tell her that he suspected Frank Hunt had killed the Durham bull and burned the barn. He didn't want to hurt her. If she really did care for Hunt, that could hurt plenty. With a shrug, he said, "Him and me don't like each other much."

She cocked a questioning brow at him.

"You like Hunt a lot, don't you?" he asked her.

A corner of her mouth quirked. "He thinks so."

Surprised, he said, "Don't you?"

"In a way," she admitted. "It's fun having him court me the way he does. But I don't think I'd want to be married to him. Not for ever and ever."

"You've been letting him think you'd marry him."

"No. I've told him I couldn't decide yet. I — well — he's the only man ever courted me, except the cowboys who come a season and go again, and don't want to settle down. They're not courting for real. They just want some fun for a while, and then to ride off free again."

Suddenly she wheeled away from Brian as if to hide her face from him. And she was crying.

His hands wanted to touch her and comfort her. He knew he ought to keep them away from her. After all, she was the boss's daughter and he was just another of those cowboys who would stay a season and be gone again. But his hands insisted. They reached out. One went to her shoulder. At the feel of it, she turned toward him. And then she was in his arms with her face against his chest.

For a moment, she was soft and warm against him. He held her gently, wanting the words to ease her sorrow, but unable to find them. His hand stroked her back. Then, as suddenly as she had come to him, she was pulling away.

154

"You're all alike!" she gasped. "You're nothing but a bunch of drifters!"

He didn't know what to say. He couldn't sort his own feelings. He stood empty-handed and uncertain, looking at her as she grabbed a poker and prodded the coals under the Dutch oven.

The silence between them grew. It was making him damned uncomfortable. He hunted a way to break it. He couldn't find the words.

Laurie spoke. Her voice was tearful and awkward. "Pa wants to see you."

"Yes, ma'am," he mumbled, knowing she was sending him away from her. He took a swallow of coffee. Carrying the cup, he went on into the bedroom.

Stone Knife lay limp on the pallet spread at the foot of Sam's bed. At his side, seated crosslegged on the floor, Bent Knee rested his chin on his chest. The hands holding the rifle on his knees were loose. His shoulders slumped. He seemed to be dozing.

In the bed, Sam was covered to the neck with a quilt. His head was sunk deep into a feather pillow. Skin pale, cheeks sunken, jowls sagging, he looked like he had aged years since Brian first saw him. His eyes were closed and for a moment Brian thought he was asleep too. But as Brian started to turn away, Sam's eyelids opened.

"Brian?" he said.

"Uh-huh?" Brian turned to face him again.

"That coffee you got there, boy?"

"Yeah." He held out the cup. "You want some?"

"I'd be obliged."

Sam looked too weak and sickly to handle the cup for himself. Brian slipped a hand under his head, helping him lift it, and held the cup to his lips. Sam got himself a long swallow. Brian moved the cup away. With a sigh, Sam said, "I feel like a newdropped calf. Hell of a thing to be so damned helpless."

"More?" Brian asked.

Sam nodded.

Holding the cup for him, Brian said, "You want to talk to me?"

The coffee seemed to give Sam strength. His voice grew firmer as he replied, "Boy, when you brought these Indians here, you have any notion you were putting my family into danger?"

"I thought about it," Brian admitted. "Only it didn't seem like much of a danger. Bent Knee there strikes me as a decent sort. He sure don't like the notion of soldiers. I figured he wouldn't make any trouble as long as Stone Knife didn't die."

"What if Stone Knife had died?"

"Bent Knee would have settled for my scalp. I don't think he'd have hurt your womenfolk. He don't seem like the kind for that."

Sam shaped up something of a scowl. "You believe Indians are predictable?"

"I reckon there's honorable men both red and white. I think Bent Knee's one of them. Hell, boss, you're the one made friends with him in the first place. I didn't think you'd let him down when he needed help."

Suddenly Sam smiled. "I reckon you're right. I thought about it a lot last night. I figured you did what

156

I'd of done myself. Only I wanted to hear you say it and say why. I wanted to know you'd thought it out, and not just done what you could to protect your own hide without a thought for anybody else. Hildy tells me you took a bad fall yesterday."

Brian rubbed his knuckles at a bruise on his face. He said, "Saddle rigging come loose on me."

"Hildy says it looked like somebody fixed it so it would."

"There wasn't no need of her bothering you with that."

"It's my business. It's my ranch, son. Now, what's this trouble between you and Jump?"

"Ain't no trouble now. I think we got it all settled."

"Good," Sam sighed. Then he asked, "How about the work? Any trouble? Anything don't set right with you?"

"No."

"Nothing? You didn't notice nothing wrong while you were on the range bringing in the horses? I mean besides the dead bull. Hildy told me you found our bull."

Brian gave a nod. He didn't want to worry Sam while he was ailing so. But Sam seemed to know things already. Brian admitted, "We didn't spot as much beef as I reckon we should have. We run onto the Baileys and rode with them, and Ed Bailey told me the herds looked scant to him. Plenty of she-stuff and new calves but not near so many steers in the bush as he'd expect."

"Yeah," Sam muttered. He called, "Bent Knee? You awake, you damned SOB?" His tone wasn't angry but affectionate.

Bent Knee lifted his head and gave a grunt in reply.

"Tell Brian here what you told me," Sam said. "Tell him what Stone Knife said about much beef."

Bent Knee looked at Brian. Gesturing off into the distance, he said, "Stone Knife see much beef in Bad Water place."

"That's another canyon off behind Wolf Canyon, where you found Stone Knife," Sam told Brian. "We don't let the cattle range out there on account of there is bad water. But there is grass. And this time of year there would be good water in places from the snow thaws. You follow me?"

"You mean there's a herd in Bad Water Canyon that shouldn't be there?" Brian said.

"Much beef." Bent Knee spread his hands. He showed Brian his fingers, opening and closing them, indicating more than he could count. Closing his arms, he showed the beef to be bunched. "Men fire mark."

"Branding!" Brian said.

Sam nodded.

Bent Knee went on, "Stone Knife see much beef. See men. See Beef-Killer —"

"That's the one that killed our bull!" Sam interrupted.

Brian nodded.

"Beef-Killer come go ride. See Stone Knife. Shoot. Stone Knife shoot. Come go ride," Bent Knee continued. "Beef-Killer shoot Stone Knife. Him fall. Horse run. Stone Knife make hide. Beef-Killer shoot. Stone Knife shoot. Stone Knife much bad hurt.

Beef-Killer maybe hurt. Beef no belong men make fire mark?"

"Maybe not," Brian muttered.

"Damn right not!" Sam exploded, the red of anger staining his pallid cheeks. "There ain't nobody got no business branding nothing around here until roundup! Ain't got business branding nothing but calves then. The men Stone Knife saw was rustlers, Brian! Rustlers road-branding *my* beef!"

Brian nodded.

Stirring as if he meant to drag himself out of bed, Sam said "We got to get them, boy!"

"Hold on there. You ain't going after nobody." Brian held out a hand, ready to push Sam down. But Sam's own weakness and pain stopped him short. He sunk back into the pillow with a sigh.

"No, I reckon I ain't," he admitted. "But somebody's got to go after them. Will you go, boy?"

"Yeah."

"Fetch Hunt and Bailey. Bailey's got two growed sons can ride along. Hunt's got Pike Coster and he ought to have an extra man or two hired on by now. That'll make seven or eight of you —"

"Not Hunt."

Sam frowned. "Why not?"

"I don't trust him."

"How come?"

"He's the one who butchered the rigging on my saddle."

"You sure of that?"

"Fairly sure."

"Damn! Why the hell would Frank do a thing like that?"

"For one thing, he wants your daughter for his wife."

"What's that go to do — oh! Laurie got eyes for you, Brian?" Sam looked like the thought amused him.

Brian shook his head. "She ain't got no use for drifters."

"A man doesn't have to be a drifter all his life," Sam said.

Bent Knee commented, "Him-woman ride good. Cook good. Strong. Come go make good squaw."

Brian felt the heat of embarrassment rising in his face. Eager to change the subject, he said, "I'd better get going, do something about those rustlers. Bent Knee, you know how many men Stone Knife saw with the beef in Bad Water Canyon?"

Bent Knee opened a hand, showing five fingers. He added one more, then waggled another.

"Six or seven," Brian said thoughtfully. "I'll get Bailey and his sons."

"Four of you against six or seven?" Sam said.

"I reckon we'll manage."

"Ed Bailey ain't a young man no more. You ought to have more help than just him and Fletch and Teddy. You sure you don't want Hunt and his men?"

"Hell, for all I know that's Hunt and his men with the beef."

"That's a strong accusation."

"Maybe I'm wrong about Hunt," Brian allowed. "But I don't want to gamble my hide on it."

"All right. It's your hide. You do what you think is best." Sam dragged a hand from under the cover and held it out. Brian clasped it, then turned to leave. Sam called after him, "Think about it, son. A man don't have to be a drifter all his life."

Brian didn't want to think about it. He made no reply as he stalked on into the living room. Laurie was by the fire. He knew she heard him walk past but she didn't look up. He took his gunbelt from the peg and slung it on, then shrugged into his jacket. As he took down his hat, he remembered the saddle. Stepping back to the doorway, he said, "Sam, I'll need a saddle. Mine ain't fixed yet."

"Take mine."

"Obliged."

This time, as Brian passed behind Laurie, she spoke. She still didn't look at him, and her voice had a thinness to it. "You leaving without breakfast?"

"Ain't got the time," he grunted. "Where's Jump and Eddie?"

"Jump's tending the horses and Eddie's milking." She rose then and turned to face him. "What's wrong?"

"Stone Knife seen some cattle back in Bad Water Canyon. I've got to fetch them out before they drink the water. Maybe you could throw some grub into a poke for me and I can eat it on the way?"

"Are you sure that's all?" She gazed into his eyes as if she could read the whole of the trouble there. "Are you sure there's nothing else?"

"Ain't nothing to worry about," he said, heading for the door.

She followed him and stood in the doorway watching as he strode toward the corral. He could sense her gaze.

He thought she knew he wasn't admitting it all to her. She understood there was danger. She was worrying for him. Funny thing. That bothered and pleased him both at the same time.

The sun lying in the east stretched long chilly shadows across the yard. Yellow Face and Much Talk had built themselves a small fire. They huddled close to it, catching its warmth in their robes. Around them the world still held the fragile silence of early morning. Every small sound seemed distinct and somehow special. Brian could hear the crackling of the fire, the noise of the horses in the corral munching grain, the squirt of milk into a bucket behind the shed.

The hound lay relaxed in a patch of sunlight near the stoop, as if it had finally accepted the presence of the Indians. It looked up as Brian neared, and gave a hopeful wag of its tail. When he paid it no heed, it dropped its head again.

Jump had finished in the corral and was heading back to the cabin. He and Brian met in the yard, a ways from the Indians. Neither Indian seemed to have moved at all, but Brian knew both were watching curiously. And warily. They had not relaxed to the situation as well as the hound had.

Jump gave a nod toward the Indians. "How much longer you reckon they're going to be here?"

"Until Stone Knife's ready to travel. Never mind them. There's work to be done."

Jump caught undertones in Brian's voice. He knew Brian meant something more than just the saddling of horses for the roundup. "What kind of work?"

Brian told him about the cattle in Bad Water Canyon.

"You're going after them?" Jump asked.

"Yeah. I'd be obliged if you'd saddle a horse for Eddie. I want him to ride over and fetch help from the Baileys."

"What about me? I'm going with you!" Jump said defiantly, expecting Brian to refuse him.

Brian licked his lips. He didn't want to take Jump into the danger of hunting rustlers. But he didn't want to revive the trouble between them by ordering Jump to stay safe at the cabin either. He said, "It's up to you. You can go or stay, whichever you want. You can back me up. Or you can stay with your family —"

"I don't need to stay with nobody!" Jump interrupted. "I'm no baby that needs nursemaiding. I can ride and handle a gun. I can handle any damned trouble you can!"

"That's why I figured you might want to stay."

"Huh?"

"Somebody ought to be close by around here to look after your womenfolk. The way your Pa's hurt, he can't do much to take care of them."

Jump looked askance at the Indians by the fire. "You think something might happen? You think they're gonna make trouble after all?"

"No! Not unless you start it. I mean other kinds of trouble. Look, somebody burnt your barn and killed your bull."

"You think whoever did that might come around and try to make more trouble?"

Brian shrugged. "I can't say. But I do know it's gonna be time for roundup right soon. If something was to happen to me while I'm after the rustlers, your folks would be hard put to get somebody else to ride for them. You might have to handle the work yourself. If something was to happen to both of us, they'd be between one hell of a rock and a hard place."

Jump understood that. He gave a solemn nod.

Brian continued thoughtfully, "Question is, can I trust you to stay here and take care of things?"

"Sure!"

"You won't make trouble with the Indians?"

"Hell, no!"

"You understand what it could mean if you did?"

Jump didn't blurt out his answer this time. He met Brian's eyes and nodded.

Looking into the boy's eyes, Brian knew that Jump did understand. Brian held out a hand. Jump accepted it. Giving Brian a bit of a grin, he turned and headed back to the corral. His stride was steady and strong and proud.

Maybe it was responsibility that could make a man out of a boy, Brian thought as he started to the shed for Eddie. But responsibility was the rope a drifter feared and shunned. He had a flash of a thought, a sudden picture of the drifter as a kind of boy trying to shy clear of growing up. That was an embarrassing idea. It made him wonder if he really was the man he had considered himself to be.

CHAPTER
THIRTEEN

As he approached the mouth of Wolf Canyon, Brian considered waiting for the Baileys. He didn't know the land beyond this canyon, except from description. But there was no telling how long it would take Eddie to find the Bailey men, and send them after him. And no telling what might be going on in Bad Water Canyon.

He left a small pile of stones with a forked stick on top at the mouth of the canyon to show the way he'd gone, and rode on in. The canyon widened, then narrowed and twisted. At the first bend, he looked back. No sign of the Baileys yet.

Spring runoff gushed down the walls of the narrowing canyon, turning its bottom into a shallow river and filling the defile with echoes of splashing water. The ground was too wet to show any sign. The sounds of the water were a steady roar in his ears. He couldn't hear over it. He didn't like that. Riding slowly, he let the horse pick its footing while he scanned the upper edges of the canyon walls. He kept his rifle ready across his saddlebow.

The trail angled up sharply. At last it brought him to the rim of the canyon. Relieved to be out of the defile, he paused long enough to leave another marker for the Baileys.

The forest between the rims of Wolf Canyon and Bad Water Canyon was thin, with little underbrush. The going was easy. But he rode with caution. If there were guards, this was where they should be.

He caught no smell of branding nor sounds of cattle being worked. No odors of man or horse in the woods. No restless stirring suggested a careless guard nearby. The lack of sign drew him taut. Before he reached the far side of the woods, he halted. Leaving his roan tied loosely, he went on afoot.

The forest stopped suddenly at the brink of Bad Water Canyon. The wall below him was a steep drop. Off to his right, it gentled into a slope with a trail down its face. He could see cattle sign on the trail. The earth had been churned where steers had been threaded down it a few at a time. A buzzard-picked carcass showed where one had fallen and never risen again.

In the bottom of the canyon, discarded airtights glittered in the sunlight. The ashes of dead fires were dark blurs on the high ground. A random heap of bones suggested that an animal had been butchered for eating.

But the herd and the men who had held it there were gone.

Brian figured they couldn't be more than a day out. Stone Knife had seen them the day before. Likely they had moved out this very morning, no more than a few hours before he left the ranch.

166

The ground told him they hadn't driven up the same trail they had gone down. He collected his mount and rode on into the canyon, hunting their sign. Studying it, he understood that the men weren't just drifting the cattle the way they would with an ordinary drive. These animals weren't being allowed to graze as they moved. They were being hurried on at a pace meant to cover land quickly.

There was more than one reason a trail boss might move a herd in a hurry. The first day or two out, he might push them to tire them out of notions of stampeding, and to get them off familiar range so that they would tend to stay bunched. He might be so eager to get them to market that he would sacrifice some weight for an early arrival.

Or he might want to get them away from the rightful owners before anyone discovered they were missing.

Brian halted once more to leave a marker and look back. Still no trace of the Baileys. Remounting, he threw his horse into a traveling trot and set out after the herd.

The cattle had been moved on through the rough canyon country and into gentler range land. Cutting across the fringes of Pearson's range, they kept to their pace. To Brian's surprise, they seemed to be headed straight for Ade's Ridge. Straight for the pass that he had struggled through when he left Tallow Dip. That had been little more than a game trail. Even in the best of weather it had been hard traveling for pack mules. Driving a herd toward it made no sense to him.

It was midday when the sign told him he was close behind the herd. Swinging off their trail, he scrambled his mount up a sharp bank. Atop the rise, he sighted the cattle.

They were in a small grassy basin cupped around with low ridges. They were being held on the grass while the drovers nooned. It looked like about five hundred head, all beef stock ready enough to be butchered. Two riders were working a lazy holding circle. A couple of men were unpacking mules while two more readied a cookfire.

Sitting askew in the saddle, resting his aching legs, Brian gazed at them. He wished he had a pair of field glasses. Damned if they didn't look familiar. But none of them looked like Frank Hunt or Pike Coster.

The breeze was coming from behind him. Craning its neck, his horse looked around and sniffed. Brian pivoted to see what had caught its interest.

There was a rider on his back trail. A slender rider on a leggy bay. Laurie Pearson.

With a jab of his spurs, Brian sent his horse skidding back down the bank. He was well out of sight of the men in the basin. He hoped he was out of hearing too as he threw his mount into a gallop. Swerving, he avoided a flat outcrop of rock that would have rung under the hammer of iron shoes, then swung past a stand of brush and saw Laurie coming toward him.

She was traveling at a fast trot. The sight of him bursting suddenly from behind the bushes startled her. With a wince, she gave her reins a tug that brought her horse to a haunch-down stop.

She had on her boy clothes and was riding astride. Rising in the stirrups, she looked about to call out to him. He waved wildly for her to keep silent.

She understood, and swallowed the shout. Gigging her horse, she hurried to meet him.

As soon as she was close enough for him to speak softly to her, he demanded, "What the hell are you doing here?"

"Oh, Brian! I was — when I heard about the rustlers — you were all alone. I was afraid! I thought you might need help!"

"I got help coming. The Baileys are on the way."

She shook her head. "Even if they were right there at the house when Eddie got there, they'd still be hours behind you."

"They'll catch up," he said. "Now, you get on home. You hear?"

"No! I want to help you!"

"Best help you can give me is to get home where you're safe."

"I can help here. I know I can."

The Pearsons were a damned stubborn lot, he thought. She didn't look about to take his orders. She didn't look like she could be augured into going back to the safety of the cabin. He decided he would have to maneuver her out of sticking with him, the way he had done with Jump. He looked past her, scanning the land. "Best thing you can do for me is to ride back and meet the Baileys. Tell them that the herd's been nooning just ahead of here. Tell them there's six men with it —" He stopped short as he suddenly realized why those men had seemed familiar. "I know them!"

"What?"

"I know the men with the cattle. They're ranahans I gambled with and drank with back in Tallow Dip last winter."

She cocked a brow at him. "You wintered with cattle thieves?"

He shrugged. A man didn't ask the feller across the poker table from him where he got his stake. And a lot of cowboys threw a long rope a time or two without thinking much of it. He said, "Maybe you've been hanging out with cattle thieves yourself."

"What do you mean?"

"Whoever moved those cattle in and out of Bad Water Canyon seemed to know the land around here right well."

"You think they're men who've worked around here?" she said. "Frank and Pa have been hiring men during the season. Could it be some of them?" She gave him an askance look. "Drifters who'd work for a while and then ride on."

He sighed, wishing she'd change her song. He was dogbone tired of being prodded about his drifting life. He said, "You go on, find the Baileys for me, will you?"

She hesitated. Very seriously, she asked, "You think Frank Hunt is behind this rustling, don't you?"

He had hoped to avoid talking to her about that. But there was no way out of it now. He replied, "I mean to find out for sure one way or the other."

"Well, I can tell you if any of the men there rode for him. Or for Pa." She didn't seem upset by the idea that Hunt might be involved. Eager to help, she lifted rein to ride on past Brian.

He snatched her bridle, holding her back. "Where are you going? You plan to ride on into their camp and look them over?"

"I don't have to go right in with them, do I? Can't I see them without being seen? You saw them, didn't you? Where were you?"

Maybe it wouldn't be a bad idea to let her look, he thought. Maybe once she'd had her look, she'd be willing to go on back. "All right. Come on."

He led her up the bank to the vantage point from which he had looked at the herd in the basin. Halting her there, he pointed. "See? Can you tell if you know any of them?"

She frowned as she studied the men. "I'm not sure. They're too far away. I can't tell."

Brian began to name them for her. "The two riding herd are called Wade and Scotty. The four by the fire are Joe and French Willie and Caldwell and a foreign kind of feller called Diamond."

She shook her head. "There's been several men called Joe around. And a Wade. I don't recall a Scotty or a Caldwell or a Diamond."

"You think it's the same Wade or one of the Joes?"

"I'm not sure. I need a closer look. If I could get up on that ridge there, maybe I could tell." As she spoke, she gigged her horse, wheeling it to ride down the back side of the bank and onto the other ridge.

The suddenness of her move caught the attention of one of the horses with the herd. Throwing up its head, it sniffed the breeze, caught the scent of strange horses, and whinnied.

"Hey!" Brian called to Laurie. He barely kept himself from shouting it. For an instant, he was about to ride after her. But even as he reined his horse toward her, he saw one of the men by the campfire rise and point in his direction.

Laurie was safely out of sight behind the rise, but Brian had been spotted.

The men in the basin were all looking at him now. One had picked up a rifle. They didn't seem scared. Just wary.

Brian knew that if he ducked now and tried to run from them, they would be more than wary. They would be after him.

Keeping his face turned toward the basin, he looked at Laurie from the corner of an eye. She had realized something was wrong and had stopped behind the bank. She was looking back at him in question.

Quietly, he said, "They've seen me. You get out of here. Stay out of sight. Go find the Baileys and tell them what's up. I'm going down to talk to them."

"No!"

"I got to, or they'll be after me. You do what I say. Don't get me in any worse trouble than you have already."

Laurie's eyes studied him a brief solemn moment. She gave a slight nod and turned her horse toward the back trail.

He sighed. Lifting rein, he urged his horse ahead, directly toward the camp and the men who waited there.

CHAPTER
FOURTEEN

As Brian neared the camp, one of the men riding the holding circle swung off his course and headed toward him. Brian called out, "Hey, Wade? That you?"

Wade grinned and waved a hand in greeting. "Hell! Brian! Damned if it ain't Brian! I sure never figured I'd see you with the hide and hair on again!"

Brian drew up beside him. "You thought I was dead?"

"Everybody did. We found some pieces of a paint horse and a saddle pack up in Tinker's Pass. Figured maybe we'd find the rest of your outfit and you under it sooner or later."

Brian grinned back at him. "You damned near did. If I'd been six foot slower getting from under that avalanche when it started, I'd have stayed with the paint horse." He nodded at the herd. "I see you fellers got some work."

"Yeah! The best kind! Quick work and lots of money." Wade turned his horse to head back to the camp. "Come on, Brian, set and eat with us. Hey, fellers! Look what I found!"

The others greeted Brian openly and cheerfully. As he stepped down from his saddle, French Willie poured a cup of coffee and held it out to him. They had fry and

174

pan bread cooking. Gesturing at it, Caldwell said, "Howdy, Brian. Smell of my cooking bring you this way?"

"Smells good," Brian said, taking the coffee. He held the cup in his hands, but he didn't drink from it. These men welcomed him. They trusted him. That bothered him. He didn't want to come into their camp and share their food and then betray them. But he didn't want to betray his boss and the brand he rode for either.

Wade dismounted and clapped him on the back. "Well, you ain't dead, old buddy, but it don't look like you've got very far either. What's keeping you in these parts?"

"A man needs a stake to get far," Brian said, glancing at the herd. The road brand the cattle wore was a pair of linked circles. He didn't know it. But he knew the vented range brands well enough. Along with Pearson's Forked P there was some of Bailey's Box B stock, and even Hunt's Rocking H. So Hunt had thrown some of his own stock in, Brian thought. Clever. If someone caught up with the stolen beef, it would look like Hunt had been robbed along with the others.

French Willie noticed the way Brian held the cup without drinking from it. He said, "Go ahead. The coffee ain't poisoned."

"Might taste like it, but it ain't," Joe grinned.

Fighting the unpleasant feeling of playing traitor, Brian sipped the coffee.

Scotty was still out circling the herd. As he came near the camp, he swung wide and hollered, "Howdy, Brian! Good to see you alive. Hey, Wade, ain't you coming back to work?"

Wade gave a grunt. Mounting, he told Brian, "I got to do my share. I'll be back when these other vultures have et and I get relief. Hang around, huh?"

Brian nodded.

French Willie poked his knife point at the meat in the skillet. "You're gonna eat with us, ain't you, Brian?"

"You got enough there to go around?"

"Hell, yeah. If we ain't, we'll butcher a beef."

"The hell we'll butcher a beef!" Caldwell said. "If we need meat, I'll go find us a slick-eared calf. We've already lost a couple of head. All the rest of this beef's going to Tallow Dip on hoof."

"Tallow Dip?" Brian looked askance at him. "The road to Tallow Dip's around the other side of the mountains. A man can't hardly pack a mule through Tinker's Pass. You sure can't drive any herd of cattle like this through it."

"We can now!" Caldwell answered, grinning as if he had swallowed a chicken. "That avalanche up there took half a mountain down into the pass. Opened her up wide enough you could drive a Borax wagon through her. I thought you knowed about that. We come across a carcass of a spotted horse we thought was yours."

"We thought you were up there with it," Diamond said slowly and solemnly. He spoke with an accent, picking his words carefully.

"Yeah," Caldwell agreed. "We started to collect that spotted horse's bones and send them home to your mama, only we didn't know her address."

"Brian, you say you're looking for a stake?" French Willie asked.

176

"I sure wouldn't mind falling into one," Brian said. "When I lost that paint horse, I lost most of my grub and gear. Near about everything I used to pawn. I hardly had anything left but the horse I was riding and the clothes I was wearing."

French Willie turned to Caldwell. "It might be we could use another man?"

"Looks to me like there's enough of you to handle a herd this size," Brian said. He cocked a brow at French Willie and put an implication into his voice. "Or do you reckon you're going to run into trouble?"

"Might be a lot of it up in the pass," French Willie admitted, but he didn't sound like he meant gun trouble. He looked at Brian, his eyes frank. "Comes some fierce storms up there this time of the year. The beef could spook and run. It's a bad place for a run. A man could get hurt."

Caldwell pursed his lips thoughtfully. He said, "If we took Brian on, it'd mean splitting our share seven ways."

Brian caught the words *our share*. So someone else did have a share in this deal. He felt certain that someone must be Frank Hunt.

"We can afford it," French Willie said. "Hell, even after the girls take their cut, we'll be up to our tails in money."

Frowning in sudden puzzlement, Brian asked, "What girls?"

French Willie's lips spread in a wide grin. "The girls at Susie's place. A piece of this herd belongs to them. They put up the money for it."

That didn't make a lick of sense to Brian. His confusion showed in his face.

Laughing, French Willie nudged Caldwell. "Tell him! Tell him what we're into here!"

Joe and Caldwell and Diamond laughed too. Caldwell said, "Brian, you know them miners up to Tallow Dip got as hungry as hell for fresh beef during the winter. Now that the road is open, they're waiting with their hands full of gold, looking for the beef to arrive. First herd that gets there is going to be worth its weight in gold."

Brian nodded.

"They're expecting a herd up the road, same as last year," Caldwell continued. "And I reckon there's one on the way. But when we got the word about Tinker's Pass being busted wide open, the boys and me got an idea maybe we could pick up some beef this side of the ridge and get it up to town before the road herd got there. Catch the gravy ahead of them!"

"So you came on through the pass and picked up the first bunch of cattle you came to?" Brian said, putting implications into his voice again.

Caldwell nodded. French Willie and Diamond kept on grinning. Joe, hunkering by the fire, was the one who caught the implications. He scowled at Brian. "We didn't just pick them up. We bought them. For cash money."

Brian shaped a kind of grin, as if he only meant to rag them. "Where the hell would you doughguts get the money to buy all that beef?"

"That's it! That's it!" French Willie nudged Caldwell again, seeming delighted about whatever Brian was to be told next.

"The girls at Susie's," Caldwell said. "Brian, you got any notion how much gold them girls got stowed away? Hard money in their boots and their garters and down their frontsides and under the floorboards. You know Susie lets them keep half the take? Well, it was a long, long winter! It's a wonder there's a one of them can still walk!"

"You mean the girls chipped in to back you and you bought this beef with their money?"

"That's what I'm telling you, ain't it?"

"Who'd you buy it from?"

"Ranchers. Who else?"

"I mean, what ranchers?"

"The ones right around here. We're still on their range. Lordy, did we ever get a price from off them! You wouldn't believe it!" Caldwell pointed at the herd. "You see them standing there all fat and sassy? All that prime beef on the hoof! You know what we paid for it?"

"Five dollars a head!" French Willie exploded with a laugh. "You know what they'll bring us in Tallow Dip? You got any idea?"

Before Brian could reply, Joe was saying, "Thirty, forty dollars a head. Maybe more."

Brian lifted both brows. Even if their story was true and they had paid for the beef, that would be one hell of a profit.

"We give the girls half," Diamond said. "We keep half. Good money."

"Damned good," Brian agreed.

French Willie clapped a hand on Brian's shoulder and spoke to Caldwell. "We can use another man, can't we? Forty dollars a head! What did we figure that would come to?"

"Twenty thousand dollars," Caldwell answered. "Half of that's ten thousand. Split six ways, that's over sixteen hundred dollars a man."

"How much split seven ways?" Joe asked.

Diamond spoke up. "Maybe we will be losing cows in the mountains. Maybe we will be only getting thirty dollars a head."

"Maybe we won't lose none at all," French Willie grinned. "The more men we got the easier it'll be to drive. Hell, maybe we'll get them all through and get fifty dollars a head off them hungry miners for them. What does it come to, Caldwell, ten thousand dollars split seven ways?"

Caldwell was busy figuring on his fingers. After a moment, he looked up. "I make it out as something around fourteen hundred apiece."

"That's all right," Joe said.

Diamond nodded.

French Willie turned to Brian again. "What about it? You want to come along with us?"

Fourteen hundred dollars was a hell of a lot of money. At forty and found, a man could work for years and never get that much together. Brian found himself trying to picture a stack of gold eagles that would add up to fourteen hundred dollars. Ten eagles to the hundred. Fourteen stacks of ten gold eagles each. A *lot* of money.

"Hell, Brian, you ain't nothing but a drifter like the rest of us," French Willie was saying. "Where you ever going to get a chance like this again?"

"*I* ain't just a drifter," Diamond muttered. "When I get the money, I will buy land and cows. Settle down. Find a fat wife, live good. Be boss."

"That fat wife'll be the boss," French Willie said.

Contemplating the wife, Diamond grinned broadly.

The image of gold glimmered in Brian's mind. A man could have a lot of fun with fourteen hundred dollars. But the talk of a wife and home put him in mind of Hildy and Sam Pearson, and of Laurie. He licked his lips thoughtfully. The Pearsons were depending on him to pull them through a bad year. If he walked out and took a couple of hundred head of their beef with him, they'd never manage to pay their debts. Laurie wouldn't get off to that school back East. Likely she would go ahead and marry Frank Hunt for lack of any better choice. And sure as hell Brian would never see her again.

He didn't think he'd ever be able to look at his own face in a mirror again, either.

Giving a slow shake of his head, he said, "I'm obliged for the offer, but I can't take you up on it. And I can't let you take these cattle off this range either."

French Willie's grin faded into bewilderment. The others looked in question at Brian. Caldwell said, "What do you mean by that?"

"Who did you say sold you this beef?"

"A rancher."

"What rancher?"

"A man name of Frank Hunt," Caldwell said. He hooked a thumb over his shoulder toward the southeast. "He's got his headquarters back yonder a ways."

"Hunt owns the Rocking H brand you've got there. He has the right to sell you that beef. But not the rest. He's got no right to sell Forked P or Box B beef."

"He has!" French Willie protested. "He explained all about it to us. Rocking H is his brand but he runs the other brands for owners back East. The owners don't know nothing about the cow business. They're investors back East. You know how that kind are, Brian. That's why he could sell us the beef so cheap. Them owners back East got some kind of money troubles and they need cash real quick. He told us all about it."

"He showed us the brand book," Joe said. The fry he had been watching was beginning to scorch. He didn't notice. He was gazing intently at Brian, defying him to deny it. "He showed us Forked P was some feller name of Pearson and the Box B was —" He paused, trying to think of the name.

"Bailey," Caldwell supplied.

"Pearson and Bailey ain't back East," Brian said. "I'm riding for Pearson, and Bailey's on his way here right now with his sons. They're looking for rustlers that are trying to take a herd of steers off their range. They don't mean to let it happen."

"Nobody's taking this beef away from us!" Caldwell snapped. Suddenly his hand darted for the gun on his thigh.

Instinctively, Brian reached for his own revolver.

"Hold it!" Joe shouted. He was no longer hunkering by the burning meat. He had ducked for one of the saddles on the ground nearby. He snatched a rifle from the boot and came up with it in his hands. It was aimed at Brian.

Brian's fingertips barely brushed the butt of his revolver. He jerked his hand back as he looked into the muzzle of the rifle. Slowly he spread his empty hands. Cautiously, he asked, "You mean to kill me?"

Joe looked uncertain.

Caldwell gave a sad, troubled shake of his head. "We don't want nobody getting hurt. But we bought and paid for this beef in good faith. We mean to take it on to Tallow Dip. We mean to get the first beef up there and get the prime price and we ain't letting nobody stop us. Not *nobody*. You understand me, Brian?"

"It ain't just us," French Willie added. "It's the girls, too. They're depending on us. We can't let them down."

Joe nodded in agreement.

Diamond looked on with a puzzled frown. They were all talking too fast for him. He asked, "Is Brian meaning to make trouble for us?"

"I don't blame you for your feelings," Brian said. "But the beef just plain ain't yours. It ain't Hunt's to sell. You go round up all the Rocking H steers you want, and it's fine with me. You fill out your five hundred head from Hunt's stock and you got my blessings. But you're not taking anybody else's beef off this range. Savvy?"

"I'd like to oblige you," Caldwell answered. "But there ain't no time. If we was to stop now and start all over again, trying to round up a herd and road brand and all, we'd never get them to Tallow Dip ahead of the other herds. We'd lose prime money. We just can't let that happen."

"Hell, Brian, if these here steers mean so much to you, you go settle it with Hunt," Joe suggested.

"I mean to," Brian said.

"Sure," Caldwell agreed. "We got about a hundred head of Rocking H stock there, and a couple hundred each of the Forked P and Box B. That's the way Hunt told us to take them. You go take four hundred head of Hunt's brand and put them other marks on them and you'll be even."

"If I take four hundred head of Hunt's stock without proof I'm entitled to do it, I'll get my neck stretched," Brian answered. He shrugged toward the herd. "If you take four hundred head that ain't Hunt's stock, you're likely to get your necks stretched."

"We got a bill of sale," Caldwell told him.

"Will it stop a bullet? There's men on the way here now to keep you from moving that beef off this range."

French Willie looked worried. "Maybe we'd better get moving."

"Yeah," Caldwell agreed. "Come on. Clear up and get riding."

Diamond noticed the burning fry. He kicked the iron skillet off the fire. It spilled charred meat on the ground. He muttered, "Hell."

184

Joe still had the rifle pointed at Brian. He asked Caldwell, "What about him?"

"You goin to kill me?" Brian asked.

Caldwell shook his head. "I can't hardly shoot you down, old friend. And I can't leave you here to put those ranchers on the trail after us. I reckon maybe you'd better ride along with us."

"They won't need me to put them on your trail. You can't hardly hide the sign of five hundred cattle."

"We'll fight them if we have to," Caldwell said. "Same as we'd fight anybody who tried to take a herd that was ours by rights."

Hopefully, Diamond said, "If we move fast, we stay good ahead."

"You know you can't," Brian answered.

"We can try," French Willie said as he stuffed gear into a pannier. The picketed mules were still wearing their pack-saddles. Hefting the pannier, he slung it onto a saddle. "Damn that Hunt to hell," he muttered as he worked. "When we get this herd took care of, I'm coming back and settle with him."

"You'd better figure on settling with Bailey and Pearson too," Brian called to him. "You're going to owe them for four hundred head of beef you're stealing."

"We not *stealing* it!" Diamond insisted. "We have *buy* it honest!"

"You expect you can explain that to a bunch of het-up ranchers with guns in their hands?" Brian looked off at the ridges. "I hope you got a good explanation right ready. You got that bulletproof bill of sale handy now?"

"Huh?" Caldwell grunted.

"There they are." Brian nodded toward a ridge.

The men all looked that way.

As Joe's eyes left him, Brian jumped. Sidestepping, wheeling, he grabbed the barrel of the rifle. His hands closing on it, he threw his weight against it. Joe gave a yelp as the trigger guard caught his finger, wrenching hard before it came free.

Jerking the rifle out of Joe's grip, Brian swung it. Caldwell was going for his revolver. The rifle butt slammed into his arm. It hit hard enough to stagger him back. He squealed with pain.

French Willie had been lashing the kettle onto a pack-saddle. Dropping it, he dove barehanded at Brian.

Brian rammed the rifle butt into his belly.

That put Brian's back to Joe. Disarmed, Joe grabbed for the handiest likely weapon. The skillet was near his feet. He clutched the handle without remembering the skillet had just come off the fire. As his fingers touched the hot metal, he let out a screech.

Brian swung around, reversing the rifle. He got a hand on the action. His finger found the trigger. That was when he discovered the gun hadn't been cocked.

Joe stood sucking his burned fingers and glowering at Brian. Caldwell crouched, cradling the arm Brian had hit with the gun butt. Diamond stood back, his hands well away from his gun, the palms turned toward Brian.

Behind Brian, French Willie was sprawled out sucking breaths. Brian could hear his gasps. The blow to the belly would keep him disabled for at least a few minutes.

186

The rifle in Brian's hands was a Sharps sporting model. As he thumbed back the hammer, he said, "Joe, you ought to know you can't hurt anybody with one of these things if you don't cock it."

"I didn't mean to hurt anybody," Joe muttered, still licking at his fingers.

"You hurt hell out of me with it," Caldwell said to Brian. "I think you've busted my arm."

"If I did, I'm sorry about it. But you shouldn't have tried that. You throw down on a man, you've got to be ready to fight," Brian answered.

Caldwell gave a grunt. He looked toward the ridge. "You said the ranchers was up there."

"I guess I said it too early."

"You bluffed us."

Brian nodded. He glanced past Caldwell at the herd. The men guarding it had seen trouble in the camp. Wade motioned for Scotty to stay with the cattle. Throwing his horse into a lope, he headed for camp to investigate. Brian took a few steps to the side and back so that he could face and cover Wade as well as the others.

Nearing, Wade slowed from a lope to a walk. He looked bewildered by the rifle Brian was pointing toward him. He didn't try going for his gun. Keeping his hands clear, he showed he had no intention of making trouble.

"What's the matter?" he called. "Brian, what the hell are you up to?"

"He's trying to take the herd away from us," Caldwell said. "He's busted my arm."

Wade frowned. "Brian, you can't take them beefs. They're ours."

"Not all of them, they ain't."

"Huh?"

Brian explained quickly.

"That ain't fair!" Wade protested.

"Take it up with Frank Hunt. You've got a hundred head of Hunt's beef. You go on, take that. I got no argument against that," Brian said.

"But that's only a hundred head!" French Willie looked plaintively at Caldwell. "We can't make no profit on a hundred head, can we?"

"Sure you can," Brian told him. "You paid twenty-five hundred for the herd, right?"

French Willie nodded slowly.

"For a hundred head, I'd make that twenty-five dollars a head. If you get thirty a head in Tallow Dip, you'll have five hundred profit. Get forty and you'll have fifteen hundred profit."

French Willie shook his head. "We promised the girls we'd double their money."

At the same time, Caldwell was saying, "But twenty-five dollars a head is delivered railroad price."

"Augur it with Frank Hunt," Brian said.

"Dammit, Brian!" Caldwell snapped. "You won't get away with this!"

Thoughtfully, Wade said, "No, Brian's right. If we've been choused, then we've been choused. We've got to settle for what we got. At least we ain't exactly lost money on the deal."

"We ain't made any either," French Willie mumbled.

"But — but —" Caldwell sputtered. He looked to the others, wanting someone to back him up against Brian.

With a shake of his head, Diamond said darkly, "I am not a thief."

Joe nodded in agreement with Diamond, but he still glared unhappily at Brian.

French Willie looked down at his feet.

With a sigh, Caldwell said, "All right, Brian. I reckon it's your hand. But I mean to get even."

Brian felt some of the tension in him ease then. But he kept the rifle steady. "It wasn't me that dealt this hand."

Caldwell turned to Wade. "You and Scotty want to start cutting out the Rocking H steers and running the others back to range? The rest of us will come help as soon as we get the camp cleared. If it's all right with the man with the gun here."

Brian nodded. But then suddenly he said, "Hold up a minute on cutting out that beef."

Wade had started back to the herd. He stopped and looked at Brian in question.

Caldwell asked, "Why?"

"Bailey, that owns the Box B, ought to be coming along soon now. I reckon I got the right to deal for the Forked P. If you want to wait until Bailey gets here, maybe we can work something out."

"Work what out?"

"Maybe a deal on the rest of that beef. You interested?"

"Depends on the deal. What you got in mind?"

"I can't talk for Bailey. You want to wait until he gets here?"

Wade spoke up. "I'd sure like to get my seat out the saddle, and put some grub in my gut before I go riding again."

The others agreed.

"All right," Caldwell said.

French Willie returned to the mule he had been packing and began to spread out gear again. Joe hunkered by the ashes of the fire to renew it.

Caldwell turned to Brian again. "Old friend, you want to put that gun down? You got our word."

Satisfied, Brian lowered the rifle.

CHAPTER
FIFTEEN

Caldwell's arm was broken. Brian splinted it for him while the others threw together a noon meal. Joe and Diamond ate hurriedly, then went to relieve Wade and Scotty on watch over the herd. Brian sat drinking coffee with the others while Wade and Scotty ate. They talked about Tallow Dip and the good times there.

Suddenly lead slammed into the dirt in front of Brian.

Dropping his cup, Brian threw himself on the ground. He rolled, grabbing for the rifle at his side. As he caught it, he realized the shot had been a warning. A bullet meant to kill would surely have hit one of the men bunched so close together at the fire.

He came up onto his feet, facing the slope the shot had come from. Lifting his empty hands into the air, he shouted, "Hold it! Bailey! That you?"

"Brian?" a gruff voice responded.

"Yeah! Come on down! There's no trouble here. We've got some palavering to do."

Cautiously, Bailey showed himself. He had been bellied down in some light brush on the crest of the slope. He stood up stiffly. With his rifle ready, he surveyed the camp in the basin over its sights.

At the shot, the cowhands with Brian had scurried for such cover as the scattering of camp gear and the pack mules offered. Brian called to them, "Come on out! Let him see it's all right!"

One by one, they came out. They were all carrying guns, but holding them down, without threat. Bailey lowered his rifle then, and waved to someone behind the ridge he stood on. A rider came up to him leading a saddled horse. Taking the horse, Bailey mounted up. He rode toward the camp. The rider waited on the slope, watching warily.

The rider looked like one of Bailey's sons. At the distance Brian couldn't be sure which one. He figured the other one was probably hidden on the slope with a gun trained on the camp, in case this was some kind of trick. Bailey was a smart man. He was game to take his chances, but he wasn't going to be foolhardy about it.

As Bailey jogged downslope into the basin, another rider appeared on the ridge. Brian started as he recognized Laurie Pearson. Dammit, he thought, couldn't she ever obey an order?

She rushed her horse past Bailey, galloping into the camp. The look on her face was frightened. Jerking rein, she dropped from the saddle in front of Brian.

"Are you all right?" she asked breathlessly. "It looked like — I was afraid — you're not a prisoner?"

Feeling flattered by her concern but angry at her heedlessness, he said, "If I was, it'd be a fool thing for you to come in and join me!"

"Oh!" she gasped, taking his response to mean he was being held captive as bait in a trap. Face pale, she looked past him at the armed men behind him.

The cowboys grinned at her. And at Brian.

"Well, I'm not a prisoner," Brian said to her. "It happens I've decided to throw in with the rustlers. Now you're our prisoner. We'll hold you hostage until we've got this herd where we're taking it."

Horror widened her eyes. "Oh no! Brian, you can't! You mustn't!"

Wade couldn't stifle a chuckle.

Laurie darted a puzzled look at him. His face gave him away. When she looked at Brian again, her fear was gone. "You're ragging me!"

Before Brian could reply, Bailey was trotting up. He had his rifle across his saddlebow, not aimed, but handy. He, too, considered the possibility that Brian might be bait in a trap. Speaking to the men behind Brian, he said. "You know I've got more men back there with guns trained down here."

"Sure," Brian said. "But it's all right. This is no trick. It seems these men have been choused. The real thief is Frank Hunt."

"Brian, Frank's up there!" Laurie gave a nod at the ridge. "He's got men with him!"

Bailey scowled skeptically at Brian. "Frank? Hell, you're wrong. Frank's no thief!"

Brian turned to Caldwell for the answer.

"It was Frank Hunt who sold us this beef," Caldwell told Bailey. "He sold us three brands. Rocking H,

Forked P, and Box B. He said he had the right to sell them all."

"Not Box B, he didn't! That's *my* brand!" Bailey snapped. He looked back at the slope. "I've got two boys up there. But Hunt's got two men with him. If you're right . . ."

Brian knew what Bailey was thinking. If Hunt and his men took a mind, they could take Bailey's boys by surprise, then likely wipe out the men around the campfire from their vantage point. They could leave it looking like the Baileys and the rustlers had shot it out with each other, both sides losing.

The open campsite was too damned vulnerable.

Brian took Laurie's arm. He nudged her toward her horse. "Come on. We're getting away from here."

The cowhands understood. They had their horses staked nearby, saddled but loose-cinched. Scotty started to run for his.

"Easy," Brian called softly to him. "Don't act scared or they'll know something's up."

Scotty slowed his pace. The others tried to look casual as they went to collect their mounts.

"It's hard to believe such a thing about Frank," Bailey said. But he eased his horse between Laurie and the ridge, offering its body and his own to her as protection from the possibility of a shot.

Brian gave her a hand up to the saddle. He told Bailey, "Take her back to the slope. Get her to cover. Ride easy, but be ready to run."

Bailey nodded. Lifting rein, he gestured for her to come along with him.

She hesitated, looking at Brian.

"I'll catch up," he said as he started for his own horse. The cowhands had already mounted up and were riding, spreading out as they headed for cover on the slopes. So far, nothing had happened. No shots had sounded. Maybe Hunt had qualms about shooting while Laurie was present, Brian thought hopefully as he rose to his saddle. Maybe Hunt really did care enough for her to want her safe and sound.

Laurie and Bailey stayed close together, riding at an easy trot. Brian caught up quickly.

As he came alongside, he asked, "How the hell did Hunt get in on this?"

Bailey answered, "It's my doing. I hadn't no idea he might be mixed up in the rustling. Eddie brought me your message and me and the boys set out to come help you. We ran into Frank and Pike and two men Frank had hired on for roundup and we asked them to come along."

"Frank was going after Bent Knee's people," Laurie put in.

Brian frowned at her. "What? Why?"

Again, Bailey supplied the answer. "Pike said Bent Knee's bunch tried to kill him. He said they ambushed him up in Wolf Canyon yesterday. A bullet skimmed his scalp. He had his head bandaged up. It was right close for him. Frank was real upset about it. Frank likes that boy a lot. He said he meant to rid this valley of them beef-eating Indians once and for all, if he had to shoot every one of them to do it."

"Brian, do you think Pike Coster might be the Beef-Killer who shot Stone Knife?" Laurie asked.

Brian nodded. "That's just what I'm thinking."

"I wanted to warn Mister Bailey that you didn't trust Frank, but I didn't have a chance," Laurie said. "And I was afraid — I didn't know what would happen if Frank went on to Bent Knee's camp. There are women and children there. It could have been awful. I thought it would be better if Frank stayed with us. I —"

"*Us!*" Brian interrupted. "Dammit, why the devil didn't you go home like I told you?"

"I was worried about you."

"I can take care of myself. I don't know if I can take care of both of us. 'Specially if you can't obey an order!"

As they neared the slope, Brian looked up at the man on the ridge. It was Teddy Bailey. Brian could see no sign that Hunt and his men had made a move. He wondered what was in Hunt's mind.

"You don't have to take care of me," Laurie was saying. "I can take care of myself."

"Sure," Brian grunted.

"Oh, you! You're the orneriest man I ever met!" she snapped back at him.

Bailey grinned, but offered no comment.

They reached the slope and headed up toward the crest. Still, nothing happened.

From the corner of an eye, Brian studied Laurie. She was gazing straight ahead, her face stiff with anger. Softly, he said to her, "You see that clump of rocks off to your right? No, don't look at it. I mean, don't move your head. You see it there?"

She glanced at the rocks and gave a slight nod.

"Well, you get on over there. Get off your horse and up close into that bunch of rocks. Take your rifle with you. Stay there. Stay put. Don't do anything or go anywhere until I call for you. If *I* don't call, if it's Hunt or one of his men that comes after you, you use that rifle. You hear?"

She started to speak. She looked as if she were about to tell him again that she could take care of herself. But the serious intensity of his voice reached her. She nodded solemnly.

"Go on," he said. "You do what I tell you this time. Savvy?"

Turning her horse, she headed for the rocks. As she left him, she whispered, "Brian, please take care of yourself."

From the corner of his eye, he watched her ride off. He hoped to hell he'd be the one who called her back again.

"What do you think?" Bailey asked. They were well up the face of the slope. There was still no sign of trouble.

Brian shrugged.

From above, Teddy called, "Pa? Everything all right?"

"Yeah," Bailey replied. "Everything all right with you?"

"Sure."

"Frank?" Bailey shouted. "You close by?"

"Here!" Hunt's voice answered from off to the left.

Bailey darted a glance at Brian. His eyes said he had doubts about Hunt's guilt. He yelled, "Come on out, Frank. Call your men out. We've got some palavering to do."

"Palavering?" Hunt asked. "Not fighting?"

"No, no fighting," Bailey said hopefully.

Hunt rose from his hiding place in the brush. He shouted for his men. One appeared from well off to the left. The other rose from cover far to the right. Both had rifles in their hands.

Brian looked to Bailey. "I don't see Pike or your other son."

"Fletch is down behind the ridge holding the horses. Pike got troubled with that head wound and went on back to the ranch," Bailey said. He glanced at Hunt. "It sure don't look to me like Frank's up to anything."

"Maybe not here and now, with Laurie so close by," Brian muttered. He gestured for the cowboys spread across the slope to come on in.

Hunt came downslope to meet them. He asked, "What's all this about palavering? Don't tell me these rustlers just surrendered peaceably?"

Brian shook his head. "They ain't the rustlers."

Cocking an eye at him, Hunt said, "What do you mean?"

Hunt had his gun in his hand. Hunt's men were all holding guns. But so was Teddy Bailey. And Ed Bailey had his rifle across his saddlebow. If someone made a sudden move, someone else could have him covered quick. Tautly, Brian said, "*You're* the thief, Hunt. *You're* the one who stole those cattle."

Caldwell was coming up to Brian's side as Brian spoke. Frowning at Hunt, he grunted, "Him? No, that ain't him."

"What the hell are you talking about?" Hunt demanded of Brian.

Bailey looked askance at Caldwell. "What do you mean, that ain't him?"

"That ain't Frank Hunt," Caldwell said.

"The hell I'm not!" Hunt snapped. "What's going on here?"

Brian looked in puzzlement from Hunt to Caldwell.

"He ain't the Frank Hunt we bought that beef off of," Caldwell said. "That Frank Hunt was a young blond feller. Had a little mustache like Joe there. Kinda looked like Joe."

"He did not!" Joe protested.

Bailey turned to Brian with a face full of surprise. "Pike Coster!"

"What about Pike? Will somebody tell me what the devil you're talking about?" Hunt demanded.

"Where's Pike Coster?" Brian snapped at him.

"His head hurt so he went back to the ranch. Will you tell me what the hell you're talk —"

Brian interrupted. Ignoring Hunt's questions, he spoke to Bailey. "You'd better get these men mounted up. It looks like Pike Coster is the one we want to palaver with."

"Why?" Hunt insisted. "What's happening? Are you trying to say Pike's mixed up in this rustling?"

At the same time, Caldwell was saying, "What about our palaver, Brian? What about this deal you said you got in mind for the beef? Ain't we gonna palaver about that?"

"Yeah. Soon as Bailey gets back," Brian answered. "Come on a ways with us. We can talk while we ride."

Bailey had started on up to the crest of the ridge. At the top, he called down to the son who held the horses out of sight. Aiming a grunt of disgust at Brian, Hunt walked up the slope after Bailey. The two of them talked together while Fletch brought up the horses and the men who had been afoot mounted. Hunt was the last to step to his saddle. He rode back to Brian at Bailey's side. As they came up to him, Brian lifted rein. Caldwell swung in next to him. Together, the four of them headed downslope.

"What about it, Brian?" Caldwell said.

Brian nodded, and asked, "Bailey, you want to make a deal for the Box B beef these men have already got gathered and road-branded?"

"What kind of a deal?" Bailey asked. He squinted warily at Caldwell as he spoke.

Brian turned to Caldwell. "Right now you and the boys got four hundred head of Forked P and Box B beef down there that you've got no right to and no profit in."

Caldwell nodded morosely.

"They've got my beef, too!" Hunt said. "What about my beef?"

Brian went on talking to Caldwell. "You figure you can get thirty-five or forty dollars a head for that beef in Tallow Dip, right?"

Caldwell nodded again.

200

Bailey whistled through his teeth and commented, "That's a damned fine price."

"Suppose you go ahead and drive the beef through," Brian suggested. "Suppose I was to pay you ten cents on the dollar for every head of Forked P stock you sold?"

"Ten cents on the dollar," Caldwell repeated to himself as he calculated. "That's — uh — four dollars if we get forty. Three-fifty if we get thirty-five."

"Seven or eight hundred for you and the boys to split," Brian said.

"Split with the girls," Caldwell put in.

Brian turned to Bailey. "Would you sell your two hundred head on the same terms? Ten cents on the dollar to the drovers?"

"Seven or eight hundred dollars to drovers just to walk a couple of hundred head of beef!" Bailey said with an indignant scowl. He could hire half a dozen men for three months hard work for that.

"Over six or seven thousand to the owner," Brian pointed out. "And it ain't that easy a walk over Ade's Ridge."

Bailey considered. His scowl faded as he counted the profit in his mind. He was almost grinning when he finally said, "Yeah, I reckon so."

"Caldwell," Brian said. "You and the boys want to walk the Forked P and Box B beef to Tallow Dip and sell them for us for ten cents on the dollar?"

Caldwell looked around at the cowboys who had moved in close enough to listen.

"Ten cents on the dollar ain't near what we had in mind," Joe grumbled.

Wade said, "It's better than nothing on the dollar."

French Willie shrugged and grinned. "Hell, as long as we're moving cattle through the pass, we might as well move them all."

The others muttered agreement with him. Caldwell spoke for them. He held his good hand toward Brian. "I reckon it's a deal."

When he had shaken Brian's hand, he shook on it with Bailey.

Looking on, Hunt said, "What about me? I've got beef in that herd, too!"

"They've already paid for your beef," Brian told him. "You take it up with Pike Coster."

"Listen here — !"

"Take it up with your man, Pike."

Glancing around at the cowboys behind Brian, Hunt eased back. His eyes were dark and thoughtful as he faced ahead in silence.

Caldwell spoke to the cowboys. "You fellers get on back, get that beef moving to market. I'll catch up. I mean to see this Pike Coster feller again before I leave here."

"Hold on," Bailey said as the cowboys began to turn back to the herd. "I think you're gonna need more men than you've got."

Caldwell eyed him askance. "What you mean?"

"With that bad arm, you'll need help. I'll send one of my boys along to give a hand." Bailey smiled as he spoke. He didn't want to come right out and admit

202

he didn't exactly trust Caldwell's bunch, but it was easy to see he wanted his own rep with the herd.

Caldwell chose not to take offense. But he protested, "He ain't sharing our cut. We've been skinned down enough already."

"Don't worry. He's my boy. I'll take care of him," Bailey agreed. He called Fletch over. "You go on with the herd. I'll send Teddy out with extra horses and supplies for you once we've took care of Pike Coster."

As the cowboys and Fletch headed for the herd, Brian swung over toward the rocks where he had ordered Laurie to hide. This time it appeared she had obeyed his orders. Her horse was loose, not far away, cropping grass. She was nowhere in sight.

Cupping his hands to his mouth, he called for her. She stood up, rifle in hand. He waved for her to fetch her horse and come along.

When she caught up, he had a try at explaining to her just how important it was for her to go on home, away from the trouble they might run into when they found Pike Coster.

She objected. She argued.

They were well onto Hunt's range before she finally gave in and reined around to ride off alone.

She was one ornery-minded girl, Brian thought. But she had eventually given in. She riled him. But she pleased him, too. He couldn't help grinning to himself as he watched her go. She was handsome as hell, riding astride that way. Damned spunky. Likely she'd grow up into a real fine woman.

CHAPTER
SIXTEEN

Hunt's ranch buildings sat on a slope in a basin. The ridges to its back gave it shelter from the winter winds. The house was of fair size, built solidly of fieldstone, with deep, narrow windows. It had a spare, military look to it.

The basin in front of the house was small. The ridges surrounding it were sudden and steep. The one directly behind was a rough rock face, topped with scant scatterings of brush. It was on this ridge that the riders halted.

As they looked down into the basin, Brian asked Hunt, "You see Pike's horse there?"

Hunt's remuda had been brought in for the roundup. The corrals were full. Squinting, Hunt peered at them. He seemed reluctant to answer.

"Seems I recollect he was riding a bald-faced sorrel," Bailey suggested.

Hunt nodded and admitted, "The horse is down there."

Caldwell said, "Could be he changed horses and skedaddled."

Hunt nodded again, but he seemed to doubt it.

"That house is built like a fort," Bailey said. "If he's inside, it ain't gonna be easy to pry him out against his will."

"Yeah," Brian agreed, studying the situation. A man behind one of the windows with a rifle could pick off approaching riders. "I see one road running in but I see a lot of ways a man afoot could get in close and get a bead on the house and still stay to cover. What if we moved in real quiet like? Then when everybody's in place, one of us can try to holler him out. Maybe once he knows he's surrounded, we can talk him into giving up."

"What if he won't give up?" Hunt asked.

Brian shrugged. "Then somebody will have to cross the yard. Hold his attention while somebody else gets into the house behind him and gets the drop on him. Hunt?"

Hunt eyed him askance.

"He's your hired hand."

"Then I suppose it's my job to lure him out?"

"Yeah. Bailey, how about you go along with Hunt? Go on down to that road." Brian indicated the wagon tracks running into the basin. "Stay out of sight of the house. Hunt can try his hollering from the road. If he has to, he can ride into view of the house and you can cover him."

Bailey nodded.

Brian talked to Hunt's two new hired hands. They agreed to move on downslope and take cover at the sides of the house. Teddy would swing around toward the front, covering it at an angle to his father's gun.

Turning to Caldwell, Brian said, "We'll need somebody high up who can see us all. Somebody who can see when we're all set and signal us it's time to move."

"I'd like to be the one who goes on down and puts his gun in that bastard's back," Caldwell grumbled.

"You're in no shape with that busted arm. You stay up here, give us a sign when everybody's ready. I'll go down the back way," Brian said.

Caldwell nodded, knowing Brian was right.

Brian spoke to them all. "Everybody keep an eye on Caldwell here. You let him know when you're set and he'll let us know when everybody's ready. Right?"

Agreeing, the men started moving out.

Brian stepped off his horse and looped the reins on a bush, then checked his guns. With a revolver on his hip and a rifle in his hand, he started down the slope toward the house.

The rocky cliff face offered some cover, but it wasn't easy climbing. He still ached from the fall he'd taken. The rifle was a nuisance. He gave it up, leaving it on a ledge, using both hands to lower himself further down. As he climbed, cautiously hunting each new foothold, he wondered if Pike really was in the cabin below. There might be one hell of a fight waiting for him there. Or maybe nothing but an empty house.

Halfway down, he paused to scan the ridges. He could see Teddy and one of Hunt's hired men. The other hired man was hidden from him by an outcrop of rock. Bailey and Hunt weren't visible to him yet. He thought they should be close to the mouth of the road.

He started moving down again. Suddenly he heard a clatter of hoofs. Steadying himself, he looked back over his shoulder into the basin.

Hunt had reached the road. He was on it, racing his horse across the yard toward the house like he'd gone wild.

Bailey wasn't far behind him. But as Hunt tore into the yard, Bailey halted, staying to cover.

Brian couldn't see the front of the house from his perch. As Hunt galloped up to it, the building blocked Brian's view of him. But sounds told Brian that Hunt jerked his horse to a stop and flung himself from the saddle.

"Pike! It's me! Frank!" Hunt shouted. His spurs jangled as his boots pounded up the steps.

From within the house, Pike called back to him, "Frank? Is something wrong?"

The door slammed open.

A moment of silence.

Shots.

Three fast shots sounded within the house.

Hurriedly, Brian slummed on downslope. When he reached the bottom, he ran for the back door.

There had been no more shooting. He thought one of the two men inside the house must be dead. Which one?

He pressed himself against the door and listened. He could hear nothing within. Cautiously, gun in hand, he opened the door.

The room he looked into ran from front to back, an eating and living room with a bedroom off to each side.

A large table filled the middle of the room. Beyond it stood Frank Hunt. He was holding his revolver in front of him. It looked limp in his hand. Used. Frank Hunt looked stunned. His glazed eyes stared at something on the floor. Something cut off from Brian's view by the table.

Brian sidled around the table.

Pike Coster lay on his back on the floor. His arms were spread wide. A pistol lay close to one hand. He wasn't wearing a hat or jacket. A crude bandage wrapped around his forehead showed traces of old dried blood. Fresh red blood smeared the front of his shirt. His eyes were open and empty, his mouth slack.

Brian shifted his gun from his right hand to his left. Hunkering, he touched Coster's face. Then, with his thumb and forefinger, he closed the gaping eyes. He looked up in question at Hunt.

Hunt seemed like a man in a trance, staring at him without seeing him.

"Hunt?" Brian said softly.

Hunt blinked. His tongue flicked across his lips. His hand tightened on the revolver he held. The gun rose to point into Brian's face. For an instant, Hunt looked about to fire it.

Brian felt that instant like an icy eternity. He saw the gun muzzle, the cylinder, the noses of the remaining bullets in the cylinder, the hammer poised above the bullet in the chamber. He knew if Hunt's finger closed on the trigger there would be no escaping that bullet. He felt the pulsing of the lifeblood in his veins and knew the sudden ease with which that life could leave him.

A shout from outside broke the frozen instant. The voice was Bailey's. "Frank! Frank Hunt! What the hell happened?"

Hunt turned slowly, as if he were sleepwalking. He started to the door and reached for the knob. Suddenly he wheeled. Face pallid, almost green, he ran for the back of the house.

Brian rose. Walking around the dead man, he opened the door. His voice snagged in his throat as he called, "Hunt's all right. Coster's dead. Everybody come on in!"

He stood waiting, breathing deeply of the fresh, cool air, while they came. Bailey, on horseback, was already in the yard. He reached the house first. Brian gestured him inside. When the others arrived, they gathered around Coster's body.

"I don't know what got into Frank," Bailey said in bewilderment. "He just up and took off for the house like he'd been snakebit. I thought maybe he meant to warn Pike. Maybe help him fight us off. He was right fond of that boy."

Caldwell muttered, "I wish I'd got to him first. I wanted a word or two with him before I done him in."

"He's dead now," Brian said. "Forget it."

Caldwell started to nod. His eyes darted to the back of the room. Brian turned and saw Hunt coming in.

Hunt's face was still as pale as white ash. His eyes were red-rimmed. He looked hollow, sunk in on himself like a man just getting past a long severe illness. It hadn't been easy for him to kill Coster, Brian thought. It had hit him hard.

Hunt's mouth worked. He had trouble finding his voice. It came roughly, a weak, broken thing. "I — he drew on me. He meant to kill me."

Bailey nodded, silent in his sympathy.

Teddy, less sensitive, asked, "What did you bust loose and go tearing off to the house like that for?"

Hunt gave a slow shake of his head as he mumbled, "Pike was my friend. My hired man. My responsibility. I thought I could talk him into surrendering."

Caldwell shuffled uncomfortably. He cleared his throat. As if he were asking permission to leave, he said, "I reckon I'd better get on back to the herd."

"Yeah," Brian agreed, giving him the permission he wanted.

Bailey put a hand on Hunt's shoulder. "You going to be all right, Frank?"

"Yes."

"You want me to take care of him?"

"No. I think the boys and I can do it." Hunt indicated the two new hired hands.

The two men were standing a little apart from the others. They were men who had been drawn into a trouble that was none of their own. They looked sorry that a man had died, but glad that it was over. After all, they had only been on the ranch a few days. Pike Coster had been little more than a stranger to them.

One said, "Sure. We'll take care of him. Bury him decent."

The other nodded in agreement.

210

"If you want, I can bring my Missus over to lay him out proper. We can speak a few words for him," Bailey suggested.

"No. No, I can speak the words," Hunt said. "It's better to get it over with."

"Then I reckon the rest of us ought to get . . ." Bailey let his voice trail off, making a question of his words. He was asking if Hunt would prefer to be left alone.

"Yes," Hunt said dully.

"All right." Bailey started for the door. "Come on, Teddy. Brian. It's all done here."

The sun was lowering, gashing the basin with long shadows, when Brian and the Baileys left Hunt's ranch. The feel of coming night was already in the air. It was a dank coolness that suggested there would be fog in the hollows, maybe even rain, before morning.

For a while the three of them rode together in silence. By the time their trails parted, the sun was gone, only its afterglow lighting the way. The breeze died with the setting of the sun. The twilight brought a kind of stillness to the mountains. Day creatures nestled into dens and burrows, ready for sleep. Night creatures weren't yet about their business.

Alone, Brian rode on at a walk, resting his horse and his own weary bones. Against the silence, the soft fall of his mount's hoofs seemed unnaturally loud. Each hoof struck the earth with a measured thud, like a counting of time. A tense waiting time. The cool of forming fog touched Brian's face. A chill lay along his spine. A thought hovered at the edge of his mind.

Bailey was wrong. It wasn't all done. It didn't all fit.

Brian could understand how Pike Coster might have run into Caldwell and discovered the opportunity to turn himself a quick handful of cash. Brian could see how easy it would have been for Coster to do it while Hunt was off wasting so much time at Pearson's instead of home minding his own business. He could see Coster frightened of being found out, wanting to drive away or kill the Indians who might be able to identify him as having been with the rustled herd. He could see Coster, cornered and frightened, throwing down on Hunt at the house. He could make sense of all that.

But what about Pearson's Durham bull? What about the burnt barn? What about his own damaged saddle? He couldn't connect any of those things with the sale of the beef to Caldwell. He couldn't guess any reason Pike Coster might have had for doing them. Were they something separate and apart from the rustling? Or were they all of a piece somehow?

The twilight faded quickly. In the hollows, the dampness thickened into a heavy mist that muffled the sounds of his horse's hoofs. It beaded on his lashes and closed in around him like a blanket. He could see only a few paces through it.

The trail from Hunt's to the Pearson ranch was well used. The horse was capable of picking its way along, and eager to be home again. With the reins hanging loosely in his hand, Brian let the horse move on at its own pace.

He heard a sound. Hoof falls. For an instant, he thought he heard an echo of his own mount's travel. Almost as he thought it, he knew he was wrong. The count wasn't quite the same. There was another horse behind him. It was traveling faster than he was. A horse close behind him, and getting closer. Halting, he twisted in the saddle to look back.

He could see only fog.

Then suddenly the rider loomed as a shadow in the darkness.

"Hello?" Brian asked of it.

"Brian!" The voice belonged to Frank Hunt. It grated through Hunt's throat like rock scraping rock, cold and hard and rough-edged. "Hold it, Brian!"

Hunt had a gun. His tone said it.

Gazing at the shadow, Brian made out the shape of it. A revolver in Hunt's hand. Leveled at Brian. Close. Too damned close. In his memory, Brian could see it clearly, the muzzle pointing and the hammer poised. If Hunt fired, he could hardly miss.

Brian spread his hands out away from his body, showing them empty. Cautiously, he slipped his stirrups.

Hunt nudged his horse a step closer. He spoke in a strange way. A distant way, as if he were speaking from the depths of a dream. A nightmare. "It's all *your* doing. *You* killed Pike!"

There was something terrible about the way he said it. Something scary as hell. Brian protested, "*I* didn't do it. You shot him."

"You made me do it. If you hadn't come here, it would never have happened. I'd have had her with no trouble at all if you hadn't come here."

"*Her?*"

"She would have married me. All I had to do was keep her from going off East, and she would have given in. She would have said yes."

"You mean Laurie Pearson?"

"Of course I mean Laurie Pearson!"

Brian understood then. The pieces all came together for him. "That's why you had Pike Coster kill Pearson's Durham bull! To keep her from going East to school where she might meet other fellers she liked better than you!"

"It would have worked! With the barn burned and the bull dead and a couple of hundred beef steers gone, Sam would have been hard put. He couldn't have sent her away. He'd have had to let me lend him money just to keep going. He'd have been obligated to me. He'd have had to let me marry her then. But you had to come along, damn you, and she wants you instead of me!"

"Unh-unh. She don't give a hoot for me," Brian said. "She ain't got a lick of use for drifters."

"You're all she can talk about now," Hunt answered bitterly. "At first, when she seemed so angry with you, I thought — but then I understood. It was because she wanted you. Women! You took her from me! You made me kill Pike! That boy was like a brother to me, and you made me kill him!"

"You shot him to save your own hide," Brian said.

214

"You made me do it!" Hunt's voice rose in a wail.

Suddenly Brian knew that Hunt's finger was tightening on the trigger.

Hunt was behind Brian on his high side. Brian had twisted half around in the saddle to face him. Boots free of the stirrups, Brian sat with his right leg hanging and his left knee bent. Most of his weight was on his left thigh. It was a precarious position. He meant it that way.

As he realized Hunt was about to shoot, he threw himself back, off the horse.

The blast of the gun was a harsh flare against the fog. The sound was overwhelming for an instant. Then it was lost, swallowed up by the night.

Brian sensed the nearness of the bullet as he toppled backward. He hit the ground with a shudder.

Startled, his horse tried to bolt. But Brian had the reins tight in his hand as he fell. The shying horse was brought up short on the bit. Pivoting, it swung its rump. It rammed into the shoulder of Hunt's mount.

Already spooky, Hunt's horse began to dance. Hunt was tugging at the reins, trying to back it clear of Brian's horse. Trying to get clear for another shot at Brian.

Brian rolled onto his belly and scrambled to his feet. Keeping his head down, he dove under the belly of his horse. He came up out of the fog on the other side of Hunt.

With a jerk, Hunt twisted to turn the gun muzzle toward him. Brian's hands snatched Hunt's leg. Pulled hard.

The gun in Hunt's hand went off. Lead skimmed close over Brian's shoulder. Damned close to his head. The blast rang in his ears, filling his mind with the thought that maybe he should have gone for his own gun. Maybe he should be shooting back.

But he didn't want to kill a man. Especially not now with his memory of Pike Coster's body so vivid. And he didn't want Frank Hunt dead.

He wanted Hunt to confess in front of the Pearsons. He wanted Laurie to know the truth from Hunt himself so that there would never be any question in her mind about Hunt.

As Brian jerked Hunt's leg, Hunt's foot slipped out of the stirrup. But Hunt managed to keep his seat. He lashed down with the gun, trying to slam it against Brian's skull. At the same time, he was tugging back the hammer for another shot.

His fog-damp thumb slipped on the hammer. The pin fell suddenly against the cartridge.

The shot exploded almost at Brian's face. The sound rammed into his head like a mule kick. The roar in his ears drowned every other sound, almost stifling even his thoughts. He staggered as if he had been hit by the slug.

As he caught his balance, his hands moved by instinct. They went for Hunt's gun. One grabbed the barrel. The other clamped over Hunt's hand on the action. He threw his whole weight against the gun, trying to wrench it from Hunt's grip. Or pull Hunt out of the saddle.

Crowded and frightened, Hunt's horse squirmed under him. Brian's horse, riderless, was held only by the dragging reins that Brian had dropped. As it backed away from the shooting, it swung to face Hunt's mount. Head to head, it bared its teeth at the strange horse.

Hunt's mount was already close to panic. At the sudden threat, it reared.

For an instant, Hunt was still firm in the saddle. Brian's grip was tight on his gun hand. For an instant, Brian was being lifted off his feet. Then suddenly he was falling back. Hunt was coming out of the saddle on top of him.

Brian sprawled on his back. Hunt fell across him. Hunt's right hand was holding the gun, locked to it by Brian's grip. His left groped for Brian's face. Found it. Covered it, the palm pressing against Brian's nose. The hand was trying to cover the nose and mouth, trying to cut off Brian's breath.

Hunt was belly to belly on top of Brian. As he shoved his weight onto the hand against Brian's face, he started to rise to his knees.

He hadn't managed to completely cut off Brian's air. Gasping scant breath, Brian twisted under him. Feeling Hunt's weight ease, Brian was aware that Hunt meant to straddle him.

He slammed a knee up between Hunt's spread legs.

He didn't hear Hunt's grunt of pain. The echo of that last shot was still deafeningly loud inside his head. But he felt Hunt's pained wince. Felt the sudden uncontrollable jerking of Hunt's body.

The hand slid off Brian's face. Hunt collapsed on top of him. But Hunt wasn't done yet. Brian could feel him struggling to recover himself.

Grabbing breath, Brian suddenly let go the gun. With a rolling twist, he dragged himself from under Hunt. Hunt snatched at him, trying to hang onto him. But for the moment, there was little strength in Hunt. Jerking free, Brian started to his feet.

Hunt realized he had possession of the gun. He was attempting to cock it as he swung it at Brian's leg.

Brian kicked. His boot hit the gun hand. The hammer fell. Brian barely heard the blast, but he saw it. He saw the hand holding the gun clearly outlined in that instant of light. He slammed his boot down on it.

The ground was damp dirt. Under Brian's boot, the gun and the hand holding it sunk in.

Hunt wrenched at the gun. He used his free hand to grab for Brian's leg. Brian jumped back. Taking his full weight on his other foot, he kicked again.

His boot rammed into Hunt's face.

The hand that had clutched for his ankle flexed. It went limp. Hunt lay still.

For a while, Brian stood over Hunt, drawing deep breaths and looking down at the man on the ground, hearing only the roaring inside his own skull, feeling only the sore aching weariness of his own body.

Slowly, his cramped lungs eased and his breathing steadied. Slowly, the roar faded inside his head. Slowly, he hunkered and recovered Hunt's gun from the dirt.

He tested Hunt's face with his hands. He could feel the dampness of blood. To his relief, he felt the warmth of life. Hunt was unconscious but not dead. He would be able to talk. And he would talk. Brian was certain of that.

There were pigging strings in Brian's pocket. He bound Hunt with them, then caught Hunt's horse. It took effort to heft Hunt's limp body across the saddle. Once Hunt was secured there, Brian paused to rest again.

As he gazed into the fog, and his own thoughts, Brian wondered if Hunt could have been right about Laurie Pearson. Could she really take a serious fancy to a drifter like him?

Did he really want to be a drifter for the rest of his life?

He didn't know.

But maybe by the time Laurie got back from that school in the East, he would have decided. Maybe by then Laurie would know for sure what she wanted, too. Maybe it wouldn't be so bad to stay hired on at the Pearson ranch long enough to find out.

Collecting his horse, he swung up into the saddle. As he headed for the Pearson ranch, he said aloud, "Come on, boy. We're going home."